A PEKIN DEW

# THE
# GHOST
# ON FIREFLY
# LANE

## PAMELA MCCORD

FROM THE TINY ACORN...
GROWS THE MIGHTY OAK

### The Ghost on Firefly Lane

First Edition
Copyright © 2019 Pamela McCord

Acorn editor: Shelly Stinchcomb

Jacket design by Dane at eBook Launch

Book interior formatted by Debra Cranfield Kennedy

www.acornpublishingllc.com

Library of Congress Control Number:2019918637

ISBN-13: 978-1-947392-73-1 (hardcover)
ISBN-13: 978-1-947392-72-4 (paperback)

*This book is dedicated to my sisters Sheila and Michelle.*
*I appreciate the time and energy and love you've gifted me with.*
*It makes me happy . . .*

# CHAPTER ONE

SCOUT UNLOCKED THE COROLLA. Pulling open his door, he asked, "You guys want to go get some lunch?"

"Sure. Benny's?" Pekin asked.

"Yes!" Amber said. "I'm dying for a burger. But I'm *really* dying for a vanilla milkshake. Vanilla shakes and ketchup go great together."

"Eww," Pekin said. "You put ketchup in your milkshake?"

"Um, nooo." She shot a glare at her friend. "I can't believe I have to explain this. You put ketchup on the French fries. And you drink your milkshake. And they go *great* together."

Over lunch, the kids discussed their upcoming session with Mildew Willingham, their go-to ghost expert. She'd kindly offered to give them some tips for dealing with spirits.

"I want to ask her about crank calls," Pekin said.

"Why? Did you get one?" Scout asked.

"How did you know it was a crank call?" Amber asked.

"Oh, maybe from the way the guy started laughing like a maniac after asking if we could get rid of his ghost."

"But—"

"Then he hung up on me."

"I thought we'd get a lot of calls after, you know, people found out about us," Scout said.

"Maybe Miranda was the only ghost in Springdale," Amber said.

"Doubt it," Pekin responded.

"It's only been three weeks since we were in the news. Too soon to decide that our ghost business is going out of business," Scout said.

"All I can say is thank God it's summer vacation. Can you imagine the teasing we'd be getting if kids at school knew about us?" Amber shivered at the thought.

"I don't even want to think about that," Pekin said.

Amber dunked a French fry in the small puddle of ketchup on her plate and took a gulp of her milkshake, then she shoved the French fry into her mouth. "Umm," she said, closing her eyes, a blissful look on her face, before she folded her hands in front of her on the table and looked at her friends solemnly. "Are we ready to take on another client? Or do we need to see what else we can learn from Mildew first?"

"Well, if one turns up, we can talk about it," Pekin said.

"What about that one who left you a voicemail while we were at Miranda's funeral?" Amber asked.

"I called back and left a message, but so far I haven't heard from him again. So, nothing for us to do right now."

"I'm sorta surprised you'd even consider doing it all again," Amber said, shoving a ketchup-covered French fry in her mouth, "after we almost lost you."

"I'm not sure I'd feel quite so okay with it if I didn't know Mildew had our backs. Having someone who really knows what they're doing takes some of the scariness out of it."

"Amen," Scout said.

As if it were destined, Pekin's phone dinged. The number seemed familiar in some way, but she didn't recognize it. Still, she held up her finger for silence and tapped the Talk icon.

"Pekin Dewlap," she said in her most business-like tone, trying to appear professional in case the call was from a potential client.

Scout rolled his eyes, but Pekin waved him off.

Scout and Amber watched her as she spoke with the other person on the phone. They could hear something of the conversation, but not enough to understand. Pekin's intense face had them ready to grab the phone themselves.

"What? What?" Amber bounced in her seat.

"Shush!" Pekin glared at her friend.

"But—"

Pekin covered the phone and shushed her again.

After a moment, she ended the call and glanced at her friends. "Good grief, Amber. Chill out."

"Sorry, but we want to know what you were talking about."

"Okay, already."

"Well, who was it?" Amber asked.

"That was Archie Dwyer. He's the person who left the voicemail, and he wants to talk to us about his ghost."

Amber dropped the fry she'd been about to pop into her mouth. "Is it a good ghost or a bad one?"

"He thinks it's...she's...harmless, but troubled. She cries

a lot. Anyway, do you guys want to go over there Tuesday afternoon? He's going to text me the address."

Amber shrugged an "okay," but added, "I guess."

"Sure, but are you okay to do this, Pekie?" Scout asked.

She sighed, inwardly smiling at his concern. "I'm a little nervous, but we should hear him out. If it sounds too scary, we can say no."

"That reminds me," Pekin said, picking up the plastic bag at her feet. "You'll never guess what Elonia sent me." She pulled out a T-shirt, which she held up so Scout and Amber could see the design printed on the front. "Look. She created a logo for us."

She handed one to each of them. "Let's wear them when we go see Mildew."

MILDEW WILLINGHAM KNEW WHO was on her front porch before the doorbell rang. It was one of her many abilities. She opened the door to three solemn faces looking apprehensively at her.

"Come in," she invited, standing aside to usher them into her modest home.

"Love your T-shirts," she said, eyeing the group.

"Our first client got them for us," Pekin said, "as a thank-you gift for saving Miranda and getting rid of George Trent. Aren't they great? Of course, it was like pulling teeth to convince Scout to wear his."

"I look dumb wearing a shirt with three ghosts on it." He glanced sideways at Pekin. "But, she made me."

Pekin laughed. She pulled down the bottom of her shirt to more thoroughly display the artwork, the black T-shirt featuring three floating sheets with round eyeholes, one ghost a little taller than the other two. Beneath the three ghosts were the words, "The Ghosties."

Pekin turned around to show the back, where printed in white letters were the words "Haunted Houses Our Specialty," followed by a phone number. "Cool, huh?"

"Is that going to be your uniform?" Mildew asked with a grin. "If so, I approve."

"Oh, no. They're just for fun. We wanted to show you. Scout probably won't even wear his again. But I *love* mine."

"Me, too," Amber piped in.

Mildew stood with her hands on her hips, a smile on her face. The diminutive woman led the teens into her family room, which was surprisingly cheery for the home of a person who speaks to dead people. Not the kind of dark, musty place Pekin envisioned would cater to the afterlife.

Pekin, Scout and Amber, fresh off their first successful experience in the ghostbusting business, were at Mildew's for instruction on how to increase their abilities in dealing with the spirit realm.

Mildew motioned for them to sit, and Pekin and Amber sat forward on the couch, directing their full attention at Mildew, while Scout sank down onto a chocolate-colored beanbag, which Pekin thought was out of place in the home of a middle-aged woman. But Mildew wasn't your average middle-aged woman.

"I can't wait," Amber said, sounding giddy, which was

quite a contrast from the fear-riddled teen she'd been before they saved Miranda from wandering the halls of Elmwood Manor for eternity.

"So, what do we do first?" the practical Pekin asked, her laptop poised and ready for note taking.

Mildew drew in a big breath and blew it out. "Well, you see, the secret is to open yourselves to the possibilities."

"Huh?" Amber asked.

"You must quiet your mind, let it be free of distractions."

"How do we do that?" Scout asked.

"I believe the best way is through meditation. Do any of you meditate?"

"Um, no," Pekin said, shooting a glance at Amber, whose worried expression might have made Pekin laugh if she hadn't been sporting the same expression.

"We don't even know how," Amber added.

"As I thought. Very well, we'll start our training there. You must all assume a prone position."

"Why do we need to meditate?" Pekin asked. "Is that the best way to communicate with the spirit world?"

"It's helpful. But meditation isn't only about speaking to ghosts. It's also useful in learning to focus, helping you clear away distractions. For example, if you want to solve a problem, sometimes meditating will allow an answer to come to you. Meditation helps you get to know yourself better. Many think it's healthful because it can help you deal with stress in your life. There are too many benefits to go into now. If you want to know more, Google is a good resource."

"Oh. Okay. Do you have mats for us?" Pekin asked.

"That would be no. I'm not running a yoga studio here." Mildew tried to look stern, but a smile was peeking through. She held up her hand as she saw Amber open her mouth to comment. "Just lie down on the floor. My carpet is clean, and thick. You can each use a throw pillow for under your head."

When everyone was comfortably situated, Mildew dimmed the lights in the family room and put on soft music with a hypnotic beat.

"This feels like when we had to take naps in kindergarten," Amber said.

"It's kinda like being in a spa, though," Pekin added.

Mildew frowned. "Close your eyes, everyone." She looked around to make sure all eyes were shut. "Now, breathing is an integral part of meditation. I want you to slowly breathe in to a count of eight and then breathe out to a count of eight. Please begin."

Scout glanced at Pekin and whispered, "Why are we doing this?"

"I can hear you, Scout," Mildew said. "Trust me, this is good for you."

"Sorry," he said, closing his eyes.

She watched the kids. They shifted a little, moved their heads, frowned. Not quite relaxed. Yet.

"The point of meditation is to clear your mind. Many practitioners prefer to be in a sitting position, back straight, cross-legged. It's called the lotus position in Yoga. Personally, I like to recline, but you can decide which position is best for you. Let's start this way, though.

Now, lie quietly for a few moments. Your breathing will relax you."

She looked at her watch, then paced until she felt an adequate amount of time had passed, observing her students. Pekin, her blonde ponytail flared out above her head, was positioned next to Scout, who was half a head taller. Amber lay in the opposite direction, pink-pedicured toes up by Pekin's head, her flip-flops discarded on the floor beside her. Amber's curly auburn hair, like a soft cloud, framed her angelic face. Mildew smiled to herself. These were good kids.

"It would be helpful for each of you to have a mantra. A word or phrase to concentrate on. You silently repeat your mantra over and over, and it centers your mind."

"Like what?" Amber piped up.

"Well, a sort of universal one is 'Om,' but any word or phrase that appeals to you will work."

"What do you use?" Amber asked.

"Personally, I silently recite 'The Lord is with me' when I inhale, and 'Always' when I exhale. I'm drawn to heavenly references because I require the Lord's protection in my line of work."

Amber closed her eyes and said, "The Lord is with me."

"You don't need to say it out loud, Amber," Mildew said. "Let's give it five more minutes, and that will be enough for now." She laughed to herself as she saw Amber's lips mouthing the words. She sat on the couch and waited for the five minutes to pass, then said, "Okay, that's a good start. You can get up now."

"I'm not sure I——" Pekin started.

"Don't worry. You can't expect to be an expert at this right away. It's something you build over time. I want you to set aside ten minutes each morning or evening and practice your meditation. When you all come back next Saturday, we'll move ahead. Any questions?"

Amber shook her head. "I might have some after I try it at home, though."

Pekin tapped her chin with her finger. "Have you always been able to see ghosts?" The kids had seen Mildew's Wikipedia page, but Pekin wanted to know more. She was curious about the little woman who'd come into their lives in the middle of their first attempt at spirit removal. And thank goodness she had because she'd been instrumental in saving Pekin's life.

"That's a far cry from our discussion of meditation," Mildew said with a laugh. "But, yes, pretty much. I saw my first ghost at six."

"I was five!" Pekin said. "I saw my grandmother."

Mildew smiled. "Well, the best ones start young." She noticed Amber's crestfallen look, and added, "But anyone who applies herself can be remarkable, too." She patted Amber's knee and stood.

"Now, let's review. Today I opened the door to meditation for you. I showed you my own technique, but you may find a different one that suits you better. You can do an internet search for other ideas. When I see you next, I hope to find you all with expanded consciousness."

"But what if we——?"

"Don't worry, Amber. So long as you try, I'm sure I'll be happy with your progress." Mildew headed toward the kitchen. "Now, who wants chocolate chip cookies?"

Three voices said, "Me!"

"As if you have to ask," Scout added with a grin as he reached out to give Pekin a hand up and led the way to the kitchen.

Sitting at Mildew's round Formica table as the little medium bustled around arranging cookies on a plate and filling glasses with milk, Pekin said, "We have something to tell you."

Mildew paused and turned toward the table. "Don't keep me in suspense."

"We might have another client," Pekin said. "A man called me when we were at lunch. We're going to meet with him Tuesday."

"What did he tell you it was about?"

"He has a sad ghost," Amber said.

"Sad?"

"He said she cries all the time."

"Well, maybe you three are just what she needs to cheer her up." Mildew smiled as she set the cookies in the middle of the table and passed out the glasses of milk.

"We hope so," Scout said, "but we won't know what we're getting into until we talk to the client."

"Good luck. You know I'm here if you need my help or have any questions. And, of course, I'm very excited for you."

"Us, too," Amber said, her eyes shining. "This ghost isn't scary like George was."

"As far as we know," Scout added. "Don't get all excited until we find out what he has to say."

"Don't be such a wet blanket. I can be excited if I want to be."

Mildew raised an eyebrow at them. "Of course you can, Amber. You can each deal with the situation in the way that feels right for you."

"Tell us about your first ghost," Pekin said, once Mildew had taken a seat at the kitchen table, cookies and milk in front of them.

"Well, as I said, I was six. I was walking to church with my mother and I pointed and said, 'Look at that pretty woman in the bonnet.' My mother was confused. She couldn't see anything, you see."

"'Where do you see a woman in a bonnet, dear?' she asked.

"I pointed. 'She's there, Mama. By the tree.' She asked if I was trying to be funny and said no one was there."

"I tried to tell her that the lady was standing right there, in a long blue dress with little buttons on the front."

Mildew sighed. "She jerked my hand and told me to stop the silliness and warned me not to mention it again or there would be *consequences*. I looked back at the lady over my shoulder and waved. She waved back. My mother was annoyed at me for the rest of the day, and I never mentioned the lady again."

"That's so sad," Amber said.

"Yes, well, my mother was a church lady, you see. The church frowned on the idea of ghosts. The only spirit allowed was the Holy Spirit."

"My parents weren't super happy when I told them about my ghost business, but at least they listened to me," Pekin said.

"Although my parents were pissed when they found out what I'd been up to," Scout added.

"Mine weren't very happy either," Amber said, reaching for another cookie. "I'm lucky I'm not on restriction for the rest of the summer."

"So, your mother never knew about your abilities?" Pekin asked.

"Actually, she did know, but not until I was older."

"Did you keep seeing ghosts?" Amber asked.

"Yes, there were other incidents. At first, I thought the people I saw were real. Over time, I noticed that they weren't quite as 'solid' as other people. There was an unearthly quality to them, a shimmer, a vagueness.

"I wasn't afraid of them, exactly. The lady in the bonnet had smiled and waved. Sometimes, however, they looked at me a little too sharply. It made me want to *not* see them."

Mildew paused to take a sip of her milk. "I was still a child when the first one said *Help me*.

"I told him, 'I'm just a little girl. I don't know how to help you.'

"'*Show us how to cross over*' the ghost said."

"How scary," Amber said, her eyes big.

"I *was* scared, Amber," Mildew said. "I was confused as to what they were asking. I told him I didn't understand. After that first ghost, I would squeeze my eyes shut whenever I caught sight of a vague human-shaped shimmer."

She sighed. "I can still hear my mother telling me it's not ladylike to make a face."

Pekin nodded and said, "I guess I was lucky. My mom saw ghosts when she was a kid, so she never made me feel like there was something wrong with me."

"You *were* lucky, Pekin," Mildew continued. "I was so lonely. I had no one to talk to. Then, when I was twelve, my mother happened to see me at just the right time. I was sitting on the wrap-around porch with a book in my lap. I didn't know she was there, but, from behind the screen door, she saw me cover my eyes with my arm and say, 'Go away. I can't help you.'

"She heard me when I lowered my arm and told the ghost I didn't know how to make it cross over. And then I started to cry.

"My mother opened the screen door and sat on the porch swing next to me. She reached over and took my hand and asked me what was wrong.

"I told her I couldn't tell her. She said, 'of course you can.' And asked me why not.

"I had to remind her that she'd said to never mention... something. She squeezed my hand and asked if I could see things she couldn't.

"I was so afraid to tell her. What if she was mad? I cried harder and said yes.

"She was silent for a moment, and said, 'Do you see something now?'

"So I took a deep breath and told her about the man

standing on the porch who wanted me to help him cross over. I said, 'I don't know what that is.'"

The three kids, cookies half-eaten on their plates, watched the little round woman talk, enthralled by her story.

"I don't know if my mother thought I had a gift or a curse, but she apologized for not listening to me. She said she believed I could see the dead.

"I could barely breathe. My mother believed me." Mildew sniffled and ran a finger under one eye. "I watched her face carefully and said, 'what's crossing over, Mama?' I felt overwhelming relief that she wasn't angry with me."

Mildew sighed. She picked up a cookie then set it down again without taking a bite. "She said that when a person dies, no one knows what happens to their spirit, although churchgoers believe that if the person lived an honorable life that person's soul would go up to heaven. She said that sometimes, perhaps, a soul isn't ready to leave this plane. He has unfinished business, or he passed too soon. His spirit doesn't leave immediately and then it's lost and doesn't know how to move on. To cross over is to find your way into the light, so you can be in heaven."

Mildew spread her hands. "As you can imagine, I was in awe, and I said, 'So the man wants me to help him go to heaven?' And my mother nodded.

"I told her I didn't know how. Mother patted my hand and said that together we'd find out.'"

Amber was transfixed. She looked at Mildew with awe as if it were Justin Bieber sitting in front of her. She finally muttered, "Wow."

"So that's how you learned to cross ghosts over?"

"Oh, no. I learned from Mrs. Potts."

"Who's Mrs. Potts?" Pekin asked.

"I thought she was a gypsy. At least she looked like one, all color and bangles."

"Really? A gypsy?" Amber said.

"I don't think she actually was a gypsy. She lived in a small tidy house near a bayou in Louisiana. Gypsies are nomads, travelers. Mrs. Potts just dressed like one."

"Oh," Amber said, trying not to look disappointed.

"Or maybe she *was* a gypsy. She had a vague European accent. Possibly Romani. That's what gypsies, or Roma as they're sometimes called, speak."

"I think she was," Amber said smugly.

Mildew smiled. "Maybe she was."

"How did you find Mrs. Potts?" Scout asked.

"My mother. She took me to see her the next day."

"Your mother? How did she—"

Mildew sighed. "You're certainly full of questions today." She took a bite of her cookie. "My mother knew more about these things than I was aware of. She grew up in the English countryside, with an aunt who seemed often to talk to herself. Her own mother had whispered that her aunt was 'special,' that she talked to the dead. Mother was fascinated and spent time with her aunt when she could. Her aunt told her stories about helping lost souls go into the light and bringing forth spirits for villagers seeking comfort. After her aunt passed away, my mother convinced herself that it had all been a figment of her aunt's imagination, and the enticing stories were just stories after all. Then I opened that door again.

"How did your mother know about Mrs. Potts?" Pekin asked.

"I want to say that Mrs. Potts had been an apprentice to my mother's aunt. There was a connection of some kind. I was just a child so didn't ask."

What did Mrs. Potts say to you?" Pekin asked.

Mildew sighed. "She told me that ghosts are lost souls looking for a way home. I never forgot that. It made me feel sympathy for them instead of fear." She looked around at the three faces hanging on every word. "Someday maybe I'll tell you about her, but it's getting late and I have errands to run. Finish your milk, and we'll meet again next week." She carried the cookie plate to the kitchen sink to rinse. Over her shoulder she said, "Don't forget to meditate."

# CHAPTER TWO

*I* DON'T THINK IT'S WORKING, Amber's text to Pekin whined. *It's so boring to just lie there and count my breaths. I tried saying Om, but that was boring, too. Are you having any luck?*

Pekin: *No. I don't know what we're doing wrong.*

Amber: *How about Scout?*

Pekin: *I'm not sure, but he's good at everything so he's probably a pro by now.*

Amber: *It figures.*

Pekin: *Hey. I know. You should come over here and we can try to do it together. Maybe we can figure out what we're doing wrong. Bring your mom's yoga mat.*

Amber: *Okay. I'll come over after dinner.*

Later, lying on mats side by side, it was hard to concentrate on meditation with all the giggling Pekin and Amber engaged in as they rattled off a bunch of silly mantras.

"I know," Amber said. "Mine is going to be 'chocolate cream pie.'"

She lay on her back with her eyes closed saying "chocolate cream pie" over and over.

"I don't think that's going to work," Pekin said. "It's

going to make you think about your stomach. Actually, I'm surprised you're not repeating 'Josh Parker Josh Parker Josh Parker.'"

"Why didn't I think of that?" Amber laughed and sat up. "And I'm hungry. You don't *have* any chocolate cream pie, do you?"

"I don't think so. But I'm pretty sure we have chocolate ice cream. Will that do?"

The girls hightailed it to the kitchen and Amber found bowls while Pekin got the ice cream out.

Once situated with their ice cream, Amber said, "Since I was at the lake with my family until a couple of days ago, I feel out of the loop. How have things been going with you and Scout?"

Pekin blushed. "Good so far. Of course, it's only been three weeks and I have to pinch myself to believe it's really real. I'm still nervous around him."

"I get it. I was a total ball of anxiety when Josh asked me out, but you've known Scout for*ever*, and he likes you just the way you are. So don't change anything and you'll be fine."

"I hope you're right. I *know* you're right. I guess I'm just being silly."

"You aren't being silly. Are you ready to double date with me and Josh?"

"I'm not sure I'm ready for that yet. Scout and I went to the movies once, and that's the only date I've had with him. And I haven't dated anyone else. Other than the prom, which was kind of my first date."

"We were lucky to go to the prom, since we weren't juniors yet. But Allen and Josh were."

"And Scout. Who went with *Vanessa Dooley*."

"You know you don't have to worry about Vanessa Dooley. Scout wants you for his girlfriend."

"I know," Pekin said, her shoulders slumping. "I can't help being a little jealous, though.

"I totally understand. But I still think you and Scout should be hanging out with Josh and me. Your parents won't mind. You're almost sixteen. You're practically a woman."

Pekin laughed. "Yeah. Why don't you try that argument out on my dad?"

"Well, we could promise to have you home before your curfew. I'm sure they'll let you go. Remember, Scout saved you from the ghost of George Trent, after all."

"How could I forget?" Pekin shivered. "I don't like to think about that."

"Sorry I brought it up." Amber scooped the last bite of ice cream into her mouth and carried her bowl to the sink to rinse, followed closely by Pekin.

"I guess we should go find our inner yogi?" Amber said.

"Namaste," Pekin said. "We're probably going to fall asleep on the floor now that we're full."

# Chapter Three

THE HOUSE AT 1756 FIREFLY LANE was a modest two-story brick colonial in a quiet, leafy neighborhood. A man they assumed was Mr. Dwyer stood on the porch waving when Scout parked in front of the house.

The kids climbed out of the car and waved back as they marched up the front walkway to the porch. Hands were shaken and introductions made, and Mr. Dwyer invited them inside.

Their host was a portly man of about fifty with thinning brown-gray hair and a pleasant manner. He offered refreshments, but Pekin thanked him and let him know that they'd just come from lunch, then offered up one of her business cards.

"The Ghost Company," Archie read. "Catchy name."

"Thank you. We each have our own. With our name on it."

"Very professional."

"So, can you tell us what's happening here, Mr. Dwyer?" Pekin asked. "You mentioned you have a ghost?"

"Please, call me Archie." He scratched his head. "My wife, Edie, and I bought this house about twenty years ago. It's such a lovely neighborhood. Trees and flowers and wonderful neighbors. When we first started to hear odd noises, we ignored them as squirrels in the attic or some such."

"How do you know that's not what was causing the noises?" Scout asked.

"Because, then we saw her."

"It's a her?" Amber asked, momentarily forgetting that Pekin had mentioned that after the phone call. "What's she like?"

"She's young, maybe in her twenties, although we've never had a clear view of her. Mostly, she glides through the halls, wailing and crying."

"Is this recent?" Pekin asked.

"No. I'd say she appeared within the first year we lived here."

"Then why are you contacting us now? Did something more happen?"

"Oh, no. It's just that we didn't have anyone to call before you kids turned up. People would think we were crazy if we went around talking about having a ghost. When we read about you guys and your haunted house business, Edie and I thought it couldn't hurt to talk to you."

"Did you see our interview in the *Springdale Tribune?*" Amber asked.

"That's where we saw it," Archie said. "Edie scours the *Tribune* every week when it comes out. She showed me the article and we thought, why not?"

"Are you scared of her?" Amber asked, curious about what they might have to face.

"Not at all. It's Edie, mostly. She feels sorry for her.

She thought maybe you could find out what's wrong and then the ghost could move on."

"Does the ghost say anything, besides the crying, I mean?" Scout asked.

"She does. She asks *where's my baby*."

"Is that all?" Amber asked.

"No. She says something like *mommy's here, baby*. Or *mommy's coming*. She glides in and out of the rooms saying it over and over. When she doesn't find her baby, she shrieks and causes wind to swirl through the house. I have to admit that we were pretty unnerved by it at first, but she's never tried to harm us so we've just accepted her. Edie calls her Windy." He giggled. "Get it? Windy?"

"Yep. We get it," Scout said, thankful Miranda wasn't around to hear the silly name the Dwyers had pasted on their ghost.

"Do you know anything about the history of this house?" Pekin asked. "To give us an idea of who she might be?"

"Not really, no. The guy selling the house had already moved out of town before we bought it."

"Do you know if any of your neighbors have lived here long enough that they might have some idea if anything tragic happened in this house?" Scout asked.

"Well, let's see. The Mastersons live in the third house south of us. It's the white house with green shutters. They're old as the hills." He chuckled. "I probably shouldn't say that. It's not very nice."

"It's okay. We won't tell anyone," Pekin said. "What do you know about them?"

"It's just Pete and Claire there now. Their kids have scattered around the country. Pete and Claire must be in their late seventies. Maybe eighties. They'd been here a long time before we moved in. I think maybe Pete is getting a little case of dementia. I don't see much of him anymore. Claire, though. She's sharp as a tack. Anyway, the Mastersons are your best bet."

"Thanks. We'll probably try to talk to them at some point," Pekin said. "Can you show us around? You know, show us where you've seen...Windy?"

"Oh, sure. She doesn't come down here so we have to go upstairs." He put a hand on the bannister and glanced over his shoulder at the kids. "Follow me."

"I hope we see her," Amber said, her head swiveling as she searched for some sign that a spirit was anywhere near. "It's warm in here, though, so I guess she's not here."

Archie laughed. "I forgot about that. It does get chilly when Windy's around."

"Does she only come out at night?" Pekin asked.

"No. Sometimes we see her as we go about our business. In the daytime, I mean."

"So, how will it work, exactly?" Scout asked. "I mean, you and Edie live here, so when would you want us around?"

A door closed and barking sounded from the first floor.

"Sounds like Edie and Spike are home," Archie said with a smile. "We're up here, dear," he called down the stairwell.

"Spike?" Amber asked.

"Spike's our little terrier. He's friendly. I hope you like dogs."

Footsteps sounded on the stairs and a slender woman with a big grin on her face appeared at the top of the stairs, a comical gray and black dog, with wiry hair sticking out all over, trotting behind her. When the little dog saw the kids, it couldn't contain its excitement and rushed up to Amber before pulling back and carefully approaching again. Amber offered her hand to sniff, and Spike reached his scruffy neck out, careful not to get too near but straining to get his nose close enough to smell this new person.

Deciding she must be okay, Spike licked her hand and flopped over on his back for a tummy rub.

"Oh, my God!" Amber screeched. "He's so *cute!*"

Pekin knelt down and rubbed the little pink tummy and got hand licks in return. Scout was last to greet Spike. His wide grin as he played with the terrier made Pekin smile.

"Has Archie told you all about our ghost?" Edie asked, and quickly added, "I'm Edie by the way. Sorry. I'm just very excited to meet you all."

"We're happy to be here," Pekin said after introducing herself and her friends. "And, yes. Archie has been filling us in."

"I feel so sorry for her. Windy, I mean. She's looking for her baby and she won't ever find it. As a mother myself, I can imagine how devastating that must be for her. It would be so great if you all can bring her some closure."

"That's what we hope to be able to do," Scout said.

"Has Archie showed you around yet?" Edie asked. Her bouncy excitement reminded Pekin of Amber.

"We were just getting started when you got home," Archie said.

"Oh, good. Then I haven't missed anything." She pointed down the hall toward the back of the house. "Windy walks this hallway calling for her baby. She's always crying. It's so *sad*."

"Does she know you can see her?" Pekin asked.

"I don't think she even knows we're here. She's too focused on searching for her baby. Anyway, this is probably where you'd get a glimpse of her."

Edie led them down the hall, giving them a tour of all the bedrooms on that floor. "Sometimes she goes in and out of these rooms, always searching but never finding. I just feel so sorry for her."

The bedrooms were cheery and bright. Nothing like the dim, eerie Elmwood Manor rooms had been. Nothing about this home looked remotely like it housed a ghost.

"So, you were about to tell us how this would work, Archie," Scout said. "Since you live here, when would you want us here?"

Archie looked at Edie and smiled. "If you take this job, we're planning to go on a week-long cruise up the Hudson River. I mean, we're going on a cruise, whether you take the job or not. But, anyway.... A week should be long enough, don't you think?"

"Oh, how fun for you," Amber said. "I've always wanted to go on a cruise."

"What Amber means," Pekin said, glancing at her friend, "is that we'd love to take the job."

"That's wonderful," Edie said, clapping her hands. "We'll have a key made. You're welcome to stay here while we're gone. There are guest bedrooms so you'd be comfortable. And," she said sheepishly, "you'd be doing us a favor by watching Spike for us? He gets traumatized when we board him someplace."

"I think we can stay here. It will be fun to have a dog to play with," Amber said, then realized she should have waited to see what Pekin and Scout thought. "We should check with our parents first, though," she added in case her friends didn't want the job.

"Of course, of course," Edie replied, touching Amber's arm. "Besides watching Spike, you'd probably have the best luck late at night. So, another reason to stay here. Does that sound like something you'd be interested in?"

"It sounds good to me," Pekin said. "Unless we tell you otherwise, plan on us staying at the house with Spike. Right, guys?"

Both heads nodded in agreement.

"Just let us know when to be here."

"One thing I should tell you," Edie said. "Spike doesn't really like Windy. In fact, he's afraid of her. So you might hear him start to bark when she's around. On the plus side, he seems to be aware of her presence before we are, so you could think of him as your early warning system."

Scout laughed. "We can use one of those. No problem. We'll protect him from the big bad ghost."

"Thank you," Edie said. "Our cruise starts a week from Friday, so maybe one night next week you could all come for dinner and we'll give you the key and answer any more questions you might have."

"Sounds great," Pekin said.

SCOUT PICKED UP PEKIN FIRST and then Amber for their second training session with Mildew.

"I can't wait to tell her about the Dwyers," Amber said. "Except I'm a little worried she'll be mad because I haven't had any luck with meditating."

"I don't think I've achieved inner peace either," Pekin said, "but Mildew told us to keep practicing."

Scout was serenely pleased with himself. He'd finally managed to find an inner calm by the end of the week, a fact he'd managed to bring up with the girls more than once.

After hearing the half-hearted meditation updates, Mildew congratulated Scout and told him to keep practicing. Then, she asked about their new client.

"They want us to stay at their house for a week while they're on a cruise," Pekin said.

"And watch their dog," Amber added.

"They don't think we have to worry about the ghost harming us," Pekin said. "Because she's been there for years and all she does is cry all the time. She's just looking for her baby."

"When does the job start?" Mildew asked.

"Next Friday," Scout said. "We're going to go over there for dinner one night next week so they can give us keys and tell us how everything works."

"Everything?"

"You know, like the TV," Scout said.

"Today's session will be timely, then. We're going to concentrate on being safe. You will remember that I said a prayer to surround us with white light when we were at Elmwood? The spirit world is fraught with danger, and whatever you can do to protect yourselves is vital. Miranda was a sweet, gentle ghost, but you also saw the opposite with the murderous George Trent."

Pekin shivered at the mention of George Trent, and Scout slipped his arm around her shoulders. She looked up at him gratefully.

Mildew gave Pekin a sympathetic glance before she continued. "I never enter a situation involving spirits, even the harmless ones," she winked at Amber, "without saying a prayer asking for protection. Ghosts may not be part of heaven or hell, but they are still under God's jurisdiction. At least, that's my belief, and it's served me well and kept me safe all my life.

"I do think it would be good to examine what happened at Elmwood Manor," Mildew said. "Thankfully, all turned out well, but things could have gone very wrong. Let's recap, shall we?"

Mildew produced a notebook and flipped it open.

"Pekin, it was brilliant to think of reading a book to the ghost. You guessed correctly that Miranda, as a young girl, was lonely after being trapped in that house for a hundred years. I'm not sure that strategy will always work, but *bravo*. In this case it was exactly right. The three of you were careful to go slowly and earn Miranda's trust. I believe this will always be your best bet. Unless you have an emergency situation where the house needs to be cleared immediately, then you should tread lightly and try to get an understanding of the circumstances.

"In the case of Elmwood, you were fortunate that the homeowner was able to provide a few details to help you understand the situation you were entering. Not only did you have an idea of who the spirit was, but knowing it was a budding teenager allowed you to come up with a strategy to reach her."

"She didn't show herself right away," Amber said.

"That's not unusual. First, I believe it's unsettling for them to have someone try to contact them. They're used to not being seen or heard by the living. So, by trying to reach out to them, you're, in effect, throwing a monkey wrench into their shadowy world. The spirits are likely to be distrustful."

"I never thought of it that way," Pekin said. "I guess I thought ghosts were mostly one-dimensional, but you're saying they can be emotional?"

"Emotions are what drive them. We may not understand the why, but their actions make sense to them. They can manifest their emotions in many ways. Ghosts can be devious and scheming. They can hide or they can do their best to frighten you. Most of them are unable to do you any harm, but there are those who are able to harness their energy, like George, and they can be dangerous. It's my hope that you don't run into any of those again. At least, not until you're experienced enough to be able to deal with them."

"I hope we don't *ever* see another one," Amber said, shuddering dramatically. "I've never been so scared in my life as when George Trent attacked us and kidnapped Pekin."

"You were all very lucky. Which is why you need to arm yourselves in any way you can to keep those spirits at bay."

"Well, you already said Holy Water was out," Amber said.

"Usually, that's true. You saw how it angered George Trent's spirit when we used it on him. So, I'd keep that on the back burner. You can always cat-burgle yourself some if you need it." Mildew smiled at Amber, teasing her about the way Amber had swiped a supply of Holy Water from the church.

"She doesn't really have to steal it," Pekin said. "I mean, it's free if you want it, right?"

"True, but that wouldn't make for as good a story, would it?" Mildew said with a chuckle.

"So, then what?" Scout asked. "Normal weapons won't work, will they?"

"Probably not. So that leaves the spiritual weapons. Like prayer. You want to ask to be cloaked in white light and blessed by the Lord. You'll also want to have a healthy supply of salt for trapping a ghost in or keeping one out."

"What about sage?" Pekin asked.

"Also good. It often works. Depends on how stubborn the spirit is. Many people also do the smudging once a ghost has been cleared from a building. The smudging is to protect the cleared space so that spirit or another won't enter."

Pekin nodded, head bent over her keyboard as she took notes.

"I've written down some simple protection prayers. I believe they are very powerful, and I would suggest that you keep a copy with you to use when you're confronted by, or in the presence of, a spirit."

"Thanks," Amber said, taking the papers from Mildew and handing one to Pekin and one to Scout. "I'm really relieved to have them."

Mildew stuck her hand in her pocket, pulled out her phone and looked at the screen. "I have to take this. I'll be back in a minute."

Pekin was drawn to a bookshelf along one wall. Her eyes scanned the titles, marveling at how the volume of books made her own paranormal collection seem small in comparison. "Look, you guys. She has a bunch of books about ghosts. *Real* ghosts. Like Amityville. I wonder if she'd let me borrow any of them."

Scout stepped beside her and looked over the titles, then pulled out a notebook tucked in among the hardbound books. "This is interesting." He held the book up and read the title. *Spirit Investigation Reports.*

He flipped through the pages. "It's a rundown of her cases. I think this is something we should do. It's really professional." He pulled his laptop out of his backpack and quickly jotted down ideas from Mildew's notebook.

"Let me see, too," Amber said. She leaned around Scout to read over his shoulder.

He looked up and caught Pekin's eye. "It has the date, the address, who hired her, the entity and a post-mortem, among other things."

"Eww, *gross*," Amber said, stepping back from Scout. "Do you have to call it post-mortem?"

"I guess not. How about wrap-up? Or summary? Summary is good. Really, guys, I think we should do this. We can still prepare one for Elonia, and we can do one for Archie and Edie."

"It takes us to a whole new level," Pekin said excitedly. "Like a real business."

"Okay, then," Scout said. "We'll add the *Spirit Investigation Report* to our list of services."

Mildew came back into the room and rubbed her hands together. "So, kids, I think we've covered enough for today."

"But——" Amber started

"What I want you to concentrate on is your meditation. I can't stress how important this is to your ability to interact with the spirit world. It takes time to master meditation, which is why you must keep practicing. Any questions?"

"Yes," Pekin said, biting her lip. "How will we know if it's working?"

"That's a good question, Pekin. First, it's important to realize that meditation takes patience. With practice, you'll begin to see subtle signs. Perhaps you'll be less distracted with other thoughts. That's normal. In time, though, you should start to feel a peace, as your mind relaxes into the meditative state. Your concentration will improve, and, even when you aren't in a meditative state, you'll be more aware of your thoughts. When thoughts interrupt your process, recognize them, but then let them go. You're looking for the stillness between the thoughts."

"The stillness between the thoughts," Scout repeated. "That sounds so deep."

Mildew laughed. "That's it. That's as simple as I can make it. And that's why it takes practice, so you can recognize the stillness when you feel it."

"I can't wait to go try it again," Amber said. "I mean, I might not have recognized it was happening."

"Just do your best. Now, on your way. I have things to do today." Mildew waved them out the front door.

# CHAPTER FOUR

S EATED AT HER KITCHEN TABLE, Pekin said, "I can't wait until Friday. I'm looking forward to our new job."

"Me, too," Amber said. "I can't wait to play with Spike. His spiked collar was *so* adorable."

"Spike's not supposed to be our focus," Scout said, rubbing his hands together as he contemplated the pizza box Pekin was flipping open.

"I know," Amber said, passing out paper plates. "But I'm sure we can fit in both. By the way, Pekin, where are your parents?"

"They're having dinner at Campbell's boyfriend's house so they can meet his parents. Meaningful?" Pekin raised her eyebrows comically. "Anyway, I thought Mildew's stories about when she started seeing spirits were interesting," Pekin said. "I hope she'll tell us some more."

"What about you?" Amber asked. "Tell us about the ghosts you used to see."

"I don't know. It kinda creeps me out to think about them."

"How can it creep you out if you have a ghostbusting business?"

"Maybe we shouldn't call it ghostbusting anymore," Pekin said. "That sounds so harsh. We're trying to *help* the ghosts, not bust them."

With a mouthful of pizza, Scout said, "We only call it that among ourselves."

"Yeah, but—"

"Getting back to my question," Amber said. "How can it creep you out?"

"Kids...ghosts! Wouldn't *you* be afraid?"

"You could have told us about them," Amber pouted, as if her feelings were hurt that her friend hadn't trusted her.

"I probably should have. But my mom warned me not to tell anyone. Besides, I really didn't want to be different."

"You missed that boat," Scout said with a grin, grabbing a spare pepperoni off her plate.

"Oh, ha. You know what I mean."

"But all those times when we were watching scary movies—"

"Yeah," Scout added. "Poltergeist, Paranormal Activity, Bride of Chucky, to name a few. And don't forget Ghostbusters. And Beetlejuice! That's not even mentioning TV shows. Lots of opportunities for you to say, *Hey, guys, I can see ghosts, too.*"

"I wanted to, but I just couldn't." Pekin sighed. "You guys would have teased me, and you would have thought I was making it up."

"Possibly," Amber acknowledged. "But you can tell us now."

"I suppose. Well, I told you about the one I saw when I

was in the first grade. When that girl in my class walked right through a little boy ghost."

"Yeah, but that's all you told us about him," Amber said. "What was it like?"

"I remember being frozen in the spot, and then the ghost looked right at me. He knew I could see him, probably from the way my mouth was hanging open and my eyes were bugged out. He started floating toward me, but Mrs. Grady bent down in front of me and asked if I was okay. I was so relieved I threw my arms around her waist and asked if she could walk me to my class. When I looked back over my shoulder, the ghost wasn't there."

"That would really freak me out," Amber said, clutching her bottle of water a little too tightly.

"It did."

"Did you ever see that ghost again?" Scout asked.

"No. I worked really hard not to. I stuck close to the playground monitors or hung out in the girls' bathroom as much as I could."

"But you saw more of them?" Amber asked.

Pekin shivered at the memories. "Oh, yeah. Mostly, I ignored them. My mom said if they knew I could see them then they'd try to talk to me. No way I wanted that. I always turned my eyes away before they noticed me seeing them. Once, when we went camping, I saw an old mountain man."

"A *ghost* mountain man?" Amber's eyes were big.

"Yes. He looked kinda like Jeremiah Johnson—"

"Who?" Scout asked, pausing mid-bite.

"Some old movie my parents made me watch. About a...wait for it...mountain man. He had a fur hat and pelts over his shoulders and fur-covered boots. Like that."

"Really?"

"No, not really. God, Amber. You're so gullible."

"That's not nice, Pekin," Scout said. "She just wanted to know how you knew he was a mountain man."

"I was kidding. Sorry, Amber." She smiled sheepishly, realizing she'd taken it too far. "He had one of those Duck Dynasty beards and long stringy hair and a hat with ear flaps."

"Really?" Amber asked again, tentatively, narrowing her eyes.

"Yes, really. I swear. Anyway, he came out of the trees in front of me and was heading on up the trail. I could see through him. I don't think he knew I was there, and I immediately turned around and ran back to find my mom."

"Mmm," Amber said, pushing her plate away and licking her fingers, something she wouldn't be caught dead doing in front of Josh. "Any really scary ones?"

"Yes! There's one I'll never forget. When I was twelve, I was at the mall with my mom and she'd sent me to the girl's department while she was looking for a blender or something. Anyway, I was holding up a sweater and looking in the mirror when I saw a person behind me. Without thinking, I smiled. And then I knew it wasn't a living person. It flew in front of me. *You can see me,* it said. I tried to pretend I couldn't, but it was too late because I couldn't drag my eyes away. I backed up, but it kept coming at me, yelling and waving its arms. I dropped the sweater and ran for the appliances department, calling for my mom. She popped out from one of the aisles to see what was wrong and I ran into her arms.

"'Is it still there?' I shrieked. She started to ask what I meant, but then she knew. She rushed me out of the store. I didn't look up at all, just kept my face buried against her. When we got to the car I finally looked around and there was no sign of the ghost. I told my mom I never wanted to see another ghost." She picked at the pizza crust on her plate. "And I never did again."

"Wow," Amber said. "What did the ghost yell at you?"

"*Help me, you have to help me.*"

"Really?"

"Yes, really." Pekin grabbed another slice from the pizza box and took a bite, not looking at her friends.

"You're pretty amazing, you know that?" Scout said, ruffling her hair.

"Thanks, Scoutie, but I'm just normal."

"Normal is one thing you definitely aren't," he said. "And it's one of the things I like best about you."

She shrugged, secretly pleased at the compliment. "I'm just me."

After sending a sweet smile Scout's way, she said to Amber, "Has Josh gotten over the whole ghost thing?" It had taken superhuman strength for Amber to keep from telling her boyfriend about the ghost at Elmwood Manor until after the case was solved.

"He was skeptical when I first told him about it, but now he's fascinated. I think he wants to see a ghost."

"He should be careful what he wishes for," Scout said, between bites.

"No he shouldn't," Pekin said. "We like our ghost."

"We like *one* of our ghosts," he responded.

Pekin shuddered. "Still, I doubt he's going to run into one anytime soon."

"That's what I told him," Amber said. "You know what, guys? I think he really likes me."

"There's an understatement. You two have been inseparable since the prom."

Amber smiled and hugged herself. "I know."

Pekin glanced shyly at Scout. She still couldn't quite believe he felt the same way about her as she felt about him. Not that they'd moved any further in their relationship. They were taking it slow, trying to figure out their feelings for each other.

Scout caught her looking at him and smiled. He squeezed her hand. "Hi," he said.

Pekin blushed. "Hi," she said back.

"Aww, you guys are so cute," Amber said. "We need to double date."

"We *are* cute, aren't we," Scout said, with a laugh. The tension that had existed between him and Pekin during the weeks before the prom was nowhere in sight. Once he'd saved her from George Trent's ghost by telling Pekin he wanted to be her boyfriend, it was like a light went on and a rosy glow surrounded the two of them.

# Chapter Five

〜〜〜〜〜〜〜〜〜〜〜〜〜〜〜〜〜〜〜〜〜〜〜〜〜〜〜〜〜〜〜〜〜〜

"**Y**OU SHOULD HAVE SEEN AMBER," Pekin said to Mildew. "She can't wait to see the ghost. Can you believe it?"

"I liked Miranda," Amber said, with a frown.

"I know. I just meant, I remember when we first started our business and you hated everything about it."

"I did, didn't I?" She giggled.

The kids had stopped at Mildew's to get any final advice she might have before they headed over to Archie and Edie's.

"It sounds like an interesting job," Mildew said.

"And not too scary," Amber said, not meeting Pekin's gaze.

"She sounds like a sad ghost. I hope we can figure out how to help her," Pekin said.

"We just wondered if you might have any suggestions for us," Scout piped in.

"Well, you need to figure out who the ghost is. To do that, you need to know the house's history. You could start by checking the Recorder's office. You were smart to ask about neighbors who might have known the previous owners, so definitely check with the neighbors."

"And then what?" Amber asked.

"When you have an idea who she is, you can try to communicate with her. If you call her by her name, she might respond. She might even talk to you like Miranda did."

"Thank goodness it's a newer house. And it's *clean*. My nails were a wreck after all the work we had to do at Elonia's house," Amber declared, inspecting her perfect manicure. "Do you think we can get the ghost to leave in a week?"

"I think it shouldn't take more than a week to get the spirit to cross over, but the more research you do and information you dig up in advance, the better chance you have of success. Miranda's situation was on a whole different level. Hopefully, you don't have another one like that."

"I think my meditation is starting to work," Pekin said with a shiver, as the mention of 'Miranda's situation' brought up images of George Trent. "I've been able to sort of let go of all my thoughts. It's kind of peaceful."

"That's great," Mildew said, with a smile. "How about you, Amber?"

"I'm still working on it," she said, looking sheepish.

"You'll get there," Mildew said, patting her arm. "So, when do you start?"

"We're having dinner tomorrow night with the Dwyers, and then we officially start on Friday."

"Well, I can't wait to hear how it goes. Of course, I'm here for anything you need."

PEKIN'S PARENTS WERE LESS than thrilled that their daughter was taking on a new project. The last one had been traumatic for all involved. They gave their consent when Pekin explained that the ghost was only interested in finding her lost baby and wasn't anything like the evil George Trent. She gave a ton of reassurances to her parents that she'd be careful and that Mildew was only a phone call away.

Pekin had to dissuade them from coming along to the Dwyers' house for dinner, however.

"How professional will we look if we have our parents hovering over our shoulders? The Dwyers are *very* nice people, and they love their ghost. That's why they want to help her. They're not afraid of her. They've lived with her for decades, so, if they're not scared, you shouldn't be."

"Easy for you to say, young lady," her father Edward said. "You didn't have to experience your daughter being kidnapped by a rogue ghost."

"Maybe not," Pekin said. "But I was the victim of the rogue ghost. If I'm okay with doing this, you have to trust me that everything will be okay."

Not surprisingly, Amber and Scout had similar conversations with their own parents.

THE AROMA OF MEATLOAF filled the room, and Pekin could almost hear Scout's stomach start growling in anticipation.

"Mmm," she said. "That smells wonderful. Comfort food is always a great choice when faced with a potentially scary situation."

"You can say that again," Scout responded with a laugh.

"So, tell us about the famous Elmwood Manor case," Archie said. "That is, if you're not sworn to secrecy."

"Given that it was splashed all over the news, there's not much secret about it," Scout said, with a laugh.

"It was all Pekin's idea," Amber said. "She used to see ghosts when she was a kid and thought it would be a fabulous idea to start a ghostbusting business."

"All true," Pekin said. "Man, you should have seen Amber at the beginning. She *hated* the whole idea. I can't tell you how many times I had to listen to her say, 'I don't like ghosts.' But then she met Miranda and now she's all about the ghosts."

Amber laughed. "I'm dying to meet your ghost," she said to Edie.

"Maybe *dying* isn't the best word to use," Scout said.

"Okay. So, here's the story," Pekin said. "I wanted to do it, and I talked these two into doing it with me. Elmwood Manor was our first client. Actually, the *owner* of Elmwood Manor was our first client. Elmwood Manor was a super scary place. It had been vacant for decades because of the weird things that went on there."

"And it was really dirty," Amber said.

"Yes. Can you imagine a century of dust? Well, not a century, but a really long time. Anyway, we had to do some cleaning to even want to be in that house."

"The windows were so dirty no light came in, so we had to wash the windows."

"And all the furniture was covered with sheets. Now *that's* a scary sight," Scout said.

"Anyway," Pekin continued, "the client told us about a young girl who'd disappeared without a trace in 1918. Her body was never found. So, we figured the ghost *had* to be her. We didn't see any sign of her for a long time, but then Amber saw her through the window and freaked out."

"I didn't—"

"You *did*! And I was so jealous that you saw her and I didn't."

"You know what Pekin did?" Amber asked. "She thought the ghost, Miranda, might be lonesome after all those years. And bored. So Pekin started reading *Harry Potter* to her. And Miranda actually appeared! Then we played music for her and showed her videos and stuff and she began to trust us."

"Then we found out that her murderer was in the house with her, and he got mad when we helped Miranda get out of the house, so he snatched Pekin and disappeared with her," Scout said, squeezing Pekin's hand. "Then he took over her body and made her try to hurt us."

"Yeah. I didn't want to hurt them, but the ghost made me do it."

"And then Mildew came to help us," Amber said.

"Mildew?" Edie asked.

"Yes. She's a *real* ghost-whisperer. I mean, she's been doing it for years. Anyway, with her help, and Miranda's help, we found Pekin in a secret room, but the bad ghost, George Trent, jumped in her mind and Pekin wasn't in control of herself."

"Oh my!" Edie said.

"Yeah. And the only way we got Pekin back was when Scout told Pekin he wanted to be her boyfriend, so she fought really hard and expelled George from her brain. Because Pekin secretly liked Scout."

"Oh my *God*, Amber."

"What? It's true isn't it?"

Pekin blushed, unable to look at Scout.

Edie clapped her hands. "That's so sweet! Like a Disney movie! So, are you and Scout together now?"

Pekin's color deepened. "I—"

"We're taking it slow," Scout said. "But, yes, we're together."

Pekin smiled at him gratefully.

"What happened after that?" Archie asked.

"The evil ghost showed Pekin's mind that he'd killed three other little girls, so, when Pekin was Pekin again, she told the police and they were able to find where those children's bodies were. Oh, and they found Miranda's bones in the garden shed in the backyard."

"So Miranda crossed over?" Edie asked.

"Actually, no. She wanted to stick around for a while and have some fun since she was only a teenager and pretty much everything has changed since she died. She'll let us know when she's ready to go," Pekin said.

"Do you still see her?" Edie asked, her eyes wide.

"Yeah. She still wants to hang out with us. We kiddingly called ourselves the Ghosties, and she said she wanted to be a Ghostie, too."

"I'm sure you can help our ghost," Edie said. "This is so exciting." She rose and began clearing the dishes off the table, and the three kids hopped up to help her.

"Is there anything else you need from us?" Edie asked. "Oh, before I forget," she reached in her pocket and pulled out a key, which she handed to Pekin.

"Would you be able to speak to your neighbors, the Mastersons, and see if they'd talk to us? Archie said they were here before you moved in so maybe they'd know some of the prior owners," Pekin said.

"I'd be happy to do that. They're very nice people. I'm sure they'd love to talk to you."

"That would be great. We'll plan to come over Friday afternoon. That will give us time to do some research before then to see what we can find out about the house's history. We're really looking forward to meeting Windy."

Edie frowned. "I hope she shows up. You never know when to expect her. It would be so disappointing if you were here all week and never saw her."

"I know. Hopefully, she'll be curious about new people in the house."

"Maybe," Edie said, a skeptical look on her face. "But the only thing she cares about is finding her baby."

"Leave it to us," Pekin said. "I know we're going to be successful."

When the dishes were done, it was time to go. Archie and Edie told them goodnight and good luck, and Edie hugged everyone.

"I really like them," Amber said once they were in Scout's Corolla. "I can't wait 'til we get started."

"Me, too," Scout said.

"Are we actually going to stay there all week?" Pekin asked. "I mean, spend the night and everything?"

Amber and Scout looked at each other. "We should take it day by day," Scout said.

"Or night by night," Amber added.

"I've already talked to my mom about it," Pekin said. "She wasn't sure it was a good idea to have a coed slumber party, but I pointed out it wasn't *really* a coed slumber party." She blushed. "I told her it's not like Scout and I are spending the night together. Alone, I mean."

Scout's mouth dropped open, and he quickly turned away, concentrating on his driving.

"I'll take the middle room to keep you two apart," Amber said, enjoying the direction the conversation had taken. "And we'll all keep our doors open. You know, so you can't sneak into each other's rooms."

"Amber!" Pekin exclaimed, flustered and at a loss how to get her friend to stop talking. "Shut up!"

"Oh, come on. Like you haven't thought about it."

"That's enough, Amber," Scout said.

"I'm just kidding with you guys. Jeez! Lighten up."

"Then quit trying to embarrass us," Pekin said, crossing her arms and glaring at Amber.

"All right. I'm sorry," Amber said, throwing her hands up. "I won't tease you anymore."

"Like you can help yourself," Pekin said, uncrossing her arms. "But we forgive you. Right, Scout?"

"Sure, yeah. Whatever."

# Chapter Six

P EKIN ARRIVED AT THE FIREFLY LANE HOUSE at noon on Friday armed with information she'd found at the County Recorder's Office.

"Okay, the house was built in 1945, and the first owners were the Silvers. They sold to the Greenburgs in 1975, who sold to the Graysons in 1992. The Graysons moved out in 1997. That's when the Dwyers bought it." She bent down to ruffle Spike's furry head. The little dog was beside itself with excitement, and hopped up and down, begging for attention from anyone who wanted to give it.

Scout patted his lap and the little dog jumped up and made himself comfortable, looking at Scout in adoration.

"Anything else?" Scout asked.

"No. I think we should try to talk to the Mastersons as soon as possible. Then we can check genealogy sites online for births and deaths. With any luck, Windy will come out sooner than later."

"Should we move into our bedrooms?" Amber asked, lifting her backpack onto her shoulder.

"Sounds good. We can each pick a room and leave our stuff there for now," Pekin said. "We can order a pizza."

"We should have pizza for dinner. Let's go to Benny's for lunch," Scout said.

"I'm in," Amber said. "And I'm starving. Burgers and milkshake, yay!"

"Let me take Spike out first," Scout said after he'd dropped his gear in one of the guest rooms. He found the red leash hanging on the back doorknob and clipped it on the dog's collar, then pulled a poop bag from the stack Edie had left on the counter for them. "See you in a few minutes."

"Wait a sec," Pekin said. She was holding a piece of paper. "It's a note from Edie. It says the Mastersons are happy to meet with us and invited us for lunch on Saturday."

"That's really nice of them," Amber said. "Scout, hurry up with Spike's walk so we can go to Benny's and get back to start looking for Windy."

BURGER IN HAND, a sheepish Amber casually said, "Josh said he wanted to stop by this evening. Is that okay with you guys? You don't mind, do you?"

Pekin immediately responded, "I don't know if that's a good idea."

"Josh already knows about our ghost business, Pekie. If we're just sitting around eating pizza, what's the problem?"

"He's so curious about what we do," Amber said. "He really wanted to see a haunted house."

"There's no guarantee he'll see anything at all," Pekin

said, starting to soften on the idea. "But, okay. No problem."

"It'll be our first double date," Amber said with a big grin.

"It's not a date," Pekin responded, a little more forcefully than was necessary. "We're working."

"Oh, lighten up, Pekie," Scout said.

"WHERE DO WE START?" Scout asked when they got back to Firefly Lane after lunch.

"I think we should go through each room and see if we feel anything. You know, a chill or something," Pekin said.

"I hope she comes out," Amber said, an excited smile on her face.

"You're being awfully brave," Pekin said. "We don't know that she'll be friendly, after all."

"Geez, Pekie, are you trying to scare Amber? She's finally totally onboard and you want to scare her off?" Scout said.

"Oops," Pekin said with a laugh. "Don't worry, Amber. Windy is going to love us. Let's start upstairs, since that's where they usually see her."

As if understanding Pekin's words, Spike darted up the stairs, followed at a slower pace by the three friends. He raced around furiously in the master bedroom then rushed out, barely missing the forest of legs standing in the doorway. He repeated the action in the bedroom next to the master, giving a little bark, but, other than commenting on his antics, the kids didn't pay a lot of attention to the little dog as his tiny legs carried him down the hall into another bedroom. Until they heard him barking frantically from the back of the house and decided to see what had him excited.

"What's up, Spike?" Scout asked, bending down to pet the antsy terrier.

But Spike dodged his hand and scooted around him and down the stairs. As three sets of eyes turned to watch him go, a chill settled over the hallway.

"Is someone here?" Pekin asked, turning in a circle, searching for the source of the chill.

"Is it Windy?" Amber asked, her eyes big.

They were met by silence as the chill faded away and the hallway returned to a normal temperature.

"What happened?" Amber asked. "Why did she go away?"

"Maybe we scared her," Pekin said.

"Whatever happened, it's gone now," Scout said. "But let's go through the bedrooms again, just in case it comes back."

After a discouraging search, they tromped back downstairs to explore those rooms.

Disappointingly, it was comfortably warm in the whole house. No sign of a ghostly breeze or temperature drop.

"Well, we've got a few hours until dinnertime," Scout said. "What do we do now?"

"Should we each go in our own room and relax?" Amber asked. "Maybe we're too overwhelming for her in a bunch."

"Amber might be right," Pekin said. "We could check our phones or read or something. What time is Josh coming over?"

"I told him around six or six thirty."

"Then I think I might take a nap," Scout said.

"I want to read," Pekin said. "Although I might come back down here in a little while and watch TV or something until we're all ready."

TWO QUIET HOURS LATER, all of them were back in the living room, with the TV turned to some mindless Bravo show.

Amber looked grumpy. Or disappointed. One of those. "I thought for sure she'd want to meet us," she said.

"Me, too," Pekin said. "At least, I hoped she would."

"What time should we order the pizza?" Scout asked. "I'm kinda hungry." He scratched Spike's ears, the little dog curled up on the couch beside him, his head resting on Scout's leg.

"You're always hungry," Pekin said.

"I'm a growing boy."

Pekin rolled her eyes, but laughed. She teased him, but she adored him, too.

He ruffled her hair. "Sorry, but I had to do that."

She patted her long blonde hair and pushed it behind her ears, smiling to herself at his attention. "Then I had to do this!"

She launched herself at him and started tickling him. He

let out a surprised laugh and pulled her into a bear hug, effectively pinning her hands so she had to stop.

"Oh, my God, you guys!" Amber said. "Do you have to do that in front of me?"

"Do what?" Scout asked with a grin, as if he had no idea what she was talking about.

"Be all over each other."

"I suppose you and Josh are going to sit on opposite sides of the room?" Pekin teased.

"Yes. We're going to have a no-touching rule."

Then Amber bent over giggling. "I'm just kidding, you guys. I love seeing you into each other."

Pekin blushed. "We're not—"

"Keep telling yourself that," Amber said. "But you really are."

"Text Josh and see what time he's coming over," Scout said. "You know, so we know what time to order the pizza."

After a few moments scrunched over her phone and pinging going back and forth, Amber announced that Josh would arrive in twenty minutes. "We can order the pizza now and make Scout happy."

# Chapter Seven

~~~~~~~~~~~~~~~~~~~~~~~~~~~~~~~~~~~~~~~~~~~~~~~~~~~~~~~~~~~~~~~~

JOSH PARKER WAS TALL AND MUSCULAR, with spiky blond hair. He looked like the jock he was.

"Hey, man," he said when Scout opened the door. Josh greeted Pekin, then said, "Hey, babe" to Amber and sat beside her on the couch, slinging an arm over her shoulders.

Amber positively glowed. And Spike did his best to insert himself between them, snuggling down in the middle.

"Pizza's coming," Scout said. "You hungry?"

"Always," Josh replied. Looking around the room, he added, "So, have you seen the ghost yet?"

"Not exactly," Amber said, gently picking up Spike and setting him on the floor. "Although we think she may have been around when we were upstairs. Spike was barking like crazy."

"We haven't been here that long yet," Pekin said. "It could take her awhile to feel comfortable and show herself."

"How will you know if she's around?"

"By the chill. When there's a ghost present, the whole room gets cold."

"Cool," Josh said, then laughed at his own joke. "I hope I get to see it."

"Well, they don't always come out when we want them to. It took days before we saw Miranda. So, prepare to be disappointed," Pekin said.

"Hey, I'm just happy to be here with my girl." He squeezed Amber's shoulder.

Embarrassment heated Pekin's cheeks. She was afraid to look at Scout, uncomfortable because Amber and Josh were so comfortable and affectionate with each other. Pekin and Scout were still warily circling each other, not quite relaxed into the reality of their new relationship. She sighed, suddenly not knowing how to act in a situation she hadn't expected to find herself in. Was she supposed to pretend she and Scout were on a date? She was slightly resentful. She'd felt in control when this situation was based on the business of helping a ghost cross over. Now she was out of her element. And embarrassed.

Interrupting her inner anxiety, the doorbell rang, signaling the arrival of the pizza. She breathed a sigh of relief.

Scout touched her shoulder gently as he headed for the front door. Pekin smiled gratefully at his departing back. *I can do this*, she thought.

She was being silly. She knew Scout liked her and he knew she liked him. But it was hard slipping from being best friends into boyfriend and girlfriend. They just had to do it at their own pace. She shoved up from her chair and went into the kitchen to get paper plates and bottles of water.

Scout, wonderful Scout, sat down on the love seat with

Pekin and draped an arm over her shoulders, giving her a squeeze before he removed his arm and reached for a slice of pizza with one hand. With the other, he ruffled her hair, causing her to laugh, banishing her anxiety.

"Sorry about your hairdo," he said.

Pekin laughed again and leaned over to give him a kiss on the cheek, and grabbed her own slice of pizza.

PEKIN WAS JUST CLOSING the lid on the empty pizza box when there was a sound from upstairs. Four faces snapped toward the stairwell.

"What was that?" Josh asked, big eyed, at the same moment Spike hopped to attention, barking and growling at the stairs.

"I guess we should go find out," Pekin said, then held a finger to her lips. "Everyone be as quiet as you can."

Scout bent to give Spike a reassuring pat and made a shushing noise at the excited dog.

Pekin led the way up the stairs, trailed by Scout, Amber and Josh. She stopped at the top of the stairs, and they all paused on the second-floor landing, listening.

The sound of soft sobbing floated in the chilled air. A very faint shimmer appeared in the middle of the hallway. Josh's hand tightened on Amber's shoulder, his mouth open in amazement.

Pekin stepped forward. "Hello?"

There was no answer and the crying stopped. "We want to help you," she continued.

With a whoosh, the specter rushed the kids, its eyes black and its mouth open as an eerie scream burst forth. A startled Josh lost his balance at the top of the stairs and started cartwheeling his arms before Scout grabbed the collar of his jacket and jerked him back on his feet.

The chill lifted and the hallway was warm again. Josh was bent over taking deep breaths.

"Are you okay?" Amber asked, her face full of concern. She put her arm around him and he stood shakily and draped an arm over her shoulders.

"Bro, you should see your face," Scout said. "You look like you've seen a ghost."

"Very funny," Josh responded sarcastically once he could find his voice.

"Is that it?" Josh asked. "Will it come back?"

"I think she's afraid," Pekin said. "I doubt we'll hear anything more from her tonight."

"*She's* afraid?" Josh said. "Unbelievable."

"You *did* want to see something, right, Josh?" Amber asked, looking up at her boyfriend.

"Yeah, *something*. I don't know what it was, but I saw it."

"Come on," Pekin said, leading the group back downstairs.

"Sorry she scared you," Amber said to Josh.

"I wasn't scared." He laughed, but wouldn't meet Amber's eyes. He sat beside her on the couch and picked up the remote, reversing the "Star Wars" sequel they'd been watching to the spot before the interruption. "She tried to push me down the stairs, but it was cool, anyway."

"She kinda did," Amber said to Scout and Pekin.

Pekin shrugged. "I guess you're a hero, Scout. You saved Josh from tumbling down the stairs."

Scout gave a thumbs-up to Josh. "Glad I was there to catch you."

"Let's just watch the movie," Josh said, frowning.

Scout held Pekin's hand through the end of the movie, making her feel safe and warm. She couldn't believe they were together, after all the months she'd spent pining over him, certain he only thought of her as a friend. Life was funny like that sometimes.

When the movie was over, Josh gave Amber a kiss and said goodnight. After walking him out, she returned to the couch with a dreamy look on her face. "Isn't he great?" she asked.

Pekin laughed. "We approve."

Everyone collapsed back on the couch. After a few minutes, Pekin sat forward. "Now that it's dark out, maybe Windy will come back. Let's go explore upstairs again."

Spike seemed to understand and trotted toward the staircase.

"Spike seems awfully brave," Scout said.

"Well, he's lived with the ghost for a really long time. He's probably not afraid of it," Pekin said.

"Yeah, but he sure hightailed it down the stairs when it got cold up there," Amber pointed out.

"Maybe he knows when to be scared," Scout said, taking the stairs two at a time.

"Can you come out?" Pekin said to the air at the second-floor landing. "We only want to help you. But we can't if you don't talk to us."

"I should start singing 'Rock-a-bye Baby,'" Amber said.

"Don't you dare!" Pekin said. "Can you imagine how upset that would make her? Either she'd never show herself to us or she might start throwing stuff at us."

"Just kidding!" Amber laughed. "You really thought I'd do that?"

"How do I know? You did invite Josh over."

Amber frowned. "Are you mad about that?"

Pekin laughed. "Of course not. It was fun. Just sayin'."

"Are you two done sniping at each other?" Scout asked.

"Yep," Pekin said. "We're just messing around."

"Shall we start getting ready?" Scout asked after they'd been through all the upstairs rooms and hadn't felt a single temperature drop.

"You mean, go to bed?" Amber asked.

"I guess. It feels strange to be staying here. I'm not sure if we're just supposed to go to sleep or stay up all night waiting for something to happen."

"Maybe we should all go into our own rooms and try to get some sleep. I'm sure if anything weird happens we'll know about it. I mean, it'll get really cold."

"I know we all staked out our rooms," Amber said, "but I don't really want to be in a room in a haunted house by myself at night. Can I stay in your room?" she asked Pekin.

"Sure. The master bedroom has a king bed so there's plenty of room for both of us."

"Thank you. It's not that I'm scared," Amber said, but her big eyes gave her away.

"Of course not," Pekin said, with a laugh. "Will you be

okay, Scout, or do you need to be in our room, too?"

Pekin blushed furiously when she realized what she'd just said. Scout ruffled her hair. "I'm a guy. I can stay in my own room. Not that it wouldn't have been fun," he said, grinning. He attempted to fix the ponytail he'd messed up, and Pekin slapped his hand away with a scowl.

"Why don't you move into the bedroom right next to the master?" Amber said. "You know, just in case."

He shrugged. "Okay. No problem, since I haven't even unpacked."

# Chapter Eight

PEKIN AWOKE WITH A START, rubbing her arms. "Amber."
She shook her friend. "Wake up."

"Huh? What?" Amber mumbled, rolling over and pulling the covers over her head.

"Amber, wake up!" Pekin poked her shoulder. "Now!"

Amber groaned and sat up. "What is it?" Her grumbly sleep face reflected her irritation.

"Look." Pekin pointed toward a lamp on the dresser. "That was off when we went to bed."

Amber sat up straighter. "You're right. Do you think Scout came in and turned it on?"

"Why would he?"

"Maybe he thought we were scared." Amber's eyes reflected her determination to believe it had been Scout.

"Maybe," Pekin responded, her eyes reflecting her doubt.

"Just turn it off so we can go back to sleep," Amber said, already snuggling back into the covers.

"I'm going to take a look around," Pekin said, sounding braver than she actually felt. She tiptoed to the bedroom door and eased it open, then stuck her head out to look around.

Everything was still and quiet. She peeked into Scout's room, but he was on his side, facing away, his even breathing indicating he was asleep.

Pekin moved stealthily to the head of the stairs and looked down over the banister but all was quiet downstairs. Quiet and dark.

Carefully closing her bedroom door so as not to disturb Amber or Scout, she tried to shrug off her apprehension. She reached for the offending lamp to turn it off, but out of curiosity picked it up for a closer look. As she did, the cord slithered across the top of the dresser and the plug plunked on the wood floor.

Pekin stared at it, her mouth open. The lamp hadn't been plugged in.

"Is anyone here?" she whispered. "We just want to help you."

"What are you doing?" Amber asked from under the covers. "Come back to bed."

"Amber, the lamp isn't plugged in."

"Good. Then it won't bother us again tonight."

"You don't understand. The lamp isn't plugged in and it's still on."

"Whatever," came the response.

"Amber! Wake up right now! The lamp isn't plugged in!"

"Geez!" Amber whipped back the covers and swung her legs off the bed. She walked over to the dresser, rubbing her eyes. When she actually focused on Pekin, she let out a shriek. "That's not plugged in!"

"That's what I've been trying to tell you."

"Is everything okay in here?" Scout stuck his head in the doorway.

"Scout, the lamp's not plugged in," Amber said, bouncing up and down in her excitement.

"What are you—" He took in the scene of the two girls standing at the dresser, the lamp shining brightly between them and the cord with its unplugged plug lying on the floor. He crossed to the dresser and picked up the end of the cord.

"It has to be Windy, doesn't it?" Pekin asked.

"Probably, but I don't feel anything."

"I know. It's not cold in here now, but I think it's what woke me up a little while ago. I saw the lamp on and Amber agreed that we hadn't turned it on, so I went to see if you did but you were asleep, so I was going to go back to bed but I was curious so I went over to the lamp and picked it up and that's when the plug fell on the floor."

Scout touched the plug as he looked at the lamp, his brow scrunched in concentration.

"Let's see if we can get her to come back."

They wandered through the dark hall and bedrooms, calling out, hoping for a response, but didn't get anything.

"It would be helpful if we had a name to call her," Pekin said.

"Yeah. I don't think she'd answer to 'Windy,'" Amber said.

"I hope the Mastersons can help us tomorrow," Pekin said.

"Me, too. I don't think we're going to have any luck until we figure out what's going on here, so let's just go back to bed, okay?" Scout said.

"Scout, can you come stay in our room?" Amber asked, looking at him with puppy dog eyes. "I'm scared."

He looked from Amber to Pekin and shrugged. He disappeared through the door and in a minute was back with blankets and a pillow, which he dropped on the floor. "This okay?" he asked.

Pekin looked at Amber. "You want Scout to sleep on the floor all night?"

"If not, he'd have to climb in with us. It might be a little crowded."

Pekin blushed, hoping the dim light in the room hid her embarrassment. "Scout, I mean, you *can* sleep in here if you want to for Amber, but we'd probably be okay if you stayed in your own room and we kept our doors open."

"No," Amber screeched. "He *has* to stay in here. I'm scared."

Pekin rolled her eyes, shaking her head. "Okay. Fine. Scout, sorry about the floor."

"It's okay. I like to go camping, and this isn't any worse than sleeping outside on the ground."

"Except there aren't any stars in here," Pekin said. "You know, to make it all worthwhile."

Ignoring her, Amber scooted over to hug him. "Thanks, Scout. You're my hero."

Ten minutes later, Pekin and Amber were snuggled under the covers in the big bed and Scout was doing his best to get comfortable on the floor.

"The lamp will be our nightlight," Amber said. "I don't like the dark anyway."

WHEN THEY WOKE UP in the morning, the lamp was off. The teens showered and dressed and met downstairs in the kitchen, where no one volunteered to cook so they decided to go to Benny's for breakfast.

"Do you think there might be an attic?" Amber asked, swallowing a bite of her pancakes. "That's where we found the clues about Elmwood."

"I didn't see any stairs leading up to another floor," Pekin said.

"Maybe there's a pull-down ladder. A lot of older houses have them. We can look for one when we get back," Scout said.

"I wish we'd thought to ask Archie whether anything that might be in an attic was theirs or could have been left over from prior owners," Amber said.

"We have to find out if there actually is one before we need to worry whose stuff it is," Pekin said.

"What time are we going to the Mastersons'?" Scout asked.

"I guess around noon. Edie didn't really say."

"Then, maybe we should get back to the house and do a little snooping for an attic before we go over there for lunch."

BACK AT FIREFLY LANE, the three of them immediately tromped upstairs to search for a concealed attic. At the far end of the hallway, there was a rectangular panel in the ceiling that had been painted the same color as the ceiling, explaining why they hadn't noticed it when they previously inspected the second floor. It didn't look like it'd been opened in a really long time.

Maybe they'd get a chance to go up there and look around, as a last resort.

# Chapter Nine

B Y THE TIME THEY HEADED DOWN three houses to the Mastersons' house, they'd burned off breakfast and Scout was ready to eat again.

A frail-looking woman opened the door with a big smile. "Welcome!" she said. "You must be Archie and Edie's friends."

"We are! I'm Pekin, this is Scout and this is Amber. Are you Mrs. Masterson?"

"Yes, but you must call me Claire. Please come in."

She stepped aside and ushered them inside before leading them down a short hallway to a comfortable-looking family room. An elderly man stood when they came in.

"Pete, these are Edie's friends. Pekin, Scout and Amber."

He waved and took a shaky step toward them. Scout walked right up to him, with his hand extended. "I'm Scout."

"I'm Pete Masterson. Pleased to meet you."

Scout helped Pete sit on the couch, and Claire motioned for all of them to be seated.

"Are you hungry?" she asked.

"Always, if you ask Scout," Amber said, with a laugh.

Claire laughed, too. I've prepared sandwiches and pasta salad. I hope that's all right."

"That sounds great," Scout said.

"Then I'll bring lunch out here, so we can talk comfortably. I'll be right back."

"I'll help you," Pekin said, getting up and following Claire into the kitchen. A few minutes later they returned, arranging the tray of sandwiches and salad and plates and utensils on the large square coffee table.

"Go ahead and dig in," Claire said, as she took a seat in an armchair to the side of the couch.

"Why don't you give them trays?" Pete said in a shaky voice. He started to rise, but Claire said, "I'll get them, dear. You just stay put."

She disappeared down a hallway and appeared a minute later with her arms full of what looked like pillows. As she handed them out, it became apparent that each flowered pillow had a tray attached.

"These are cool," Amber said, adjusting hers on her lap. "I need these for my house."

"Yes," Claire said. "Our children gave them to us for Christmas a few years ago."

"More than a few," Pete mumbled as he transferred a sandwich from the coffee table to his tray.

Claire laughed. "You're right, dear. More than a few."

Once the plates were full and the munching subsided, Claire said, "So, Edie told me you were interested in the history of their house. Is that right?"

"Yes. Since we're house-sitting for them, we thought it

would be cool to know about the house. You know, how old it is, who lived there before. That kind of stuff," Pekin said.

"Edie said you've lived in the neighborhood since before they moved in so she thought you might remember some of the earlier occupants," Scout said.

"Yes, we've been here fifty years," Claire said. "We've had the pleasure of knowing two other families who lived there before the Dwyers."

"We lived in this house for fifty-two years," Pete said.

"Wow, that's a long time," Amber said. "It is a really nice neighborhood."

"What were they like, the other families?" Pekin asked Claire. "I mean, were they young families or retired people? Did they have any kids?"

"Well, let me see. She tapped a long bony finger to her lips as she thought back. When we first moved here—"

"We've lived in this house for fifty-two years," Pete said, with a smile. "It's a wonderful home."

"That's so great," Amber said.

"You already told them that, Pete," Claire said. "Remember?" She looked at him lovingly and patted his hand.

"So, anyway," Claire continued, "the Silvers were the original owners of the house. They sold it and moved, in 1975, when Ed and Marie Greenburg bought it. Such nice people. They were older, and eventually moved to Florida to be closer to Marie's sister.

"The Graysons bought the house from them. I can't remember the exact year, maybe '90, '91. Something like that."

"Did I tell you we've lived in this house for fifty-two years?" Pete said.

Claire patted his hand again. "We have, haven't we, dear. It's a wonderful home."

She looked back at the teens. "Anyway, Ron and Lily Grayson weren't here that long."

"That poor woman died," Pete said.

"What woman?" Pekin's ears perked up.

"We bought this house fifty-two years ago," Pete said, his moment of clarity receding.

"What woman?" Pekin asked again.

"He means Lily Grayson. The poor dear passed away during childbirth. In her own home."

"Why was she at home and not at the hospital?" Amber asked.

"I think her labor started suddenly and Ron was at work. She was a couple of weeks early, so no one was expecting it. She managed to call Ron and he rushed home, but by the time he got there she was too close to delivery for him to get her to the hospital. He called her doctor and did what he could to help with the delivery, but, when Lily suddenly stopped breathing after the baby was born, Ron couldn't get her back. By the time the doctor arrived, Lily was gone."

"Did the baby die, too?" Pekin asked.

"Oh, no. The baby lived, but Ron fell apart. Shortly after Lily passed away, Ron moved. He said he couldn't bear to be in the house with her gone. He put the house on the market. Had a realtor manage everything. The house sold a couple of months after Ron left."

"I don't blame him," Amber said.

"What happened to them? Do you know where they went?"

"I think Ron put in for a transfer with his job and moved to New Orleans."

"With the baby?" Pekin asked.

"Of course. I felt so sorry for that young man, having to raise a baby alone."

"Do you, um, do you know what the baby's name was?" Scout said.

"Yes. It was Violet, the name Lily had chosen for a girl."

"And you never heard from them after that?"

"No. We never did, did we, Pete?"

"Did I tell you that someone died in that house? She never got to see her baby." He looked around, seemingly confused. "What were we talking about?"

Claire gave a little laugh. "It's okay, honey. We were talking about the Graysons."

"Such a nice young family," he said. "So sad she died."

Claire looked at the kids apologetically. "I think Pete's tired. I'm going to help him to bed for a nap. I'll be right back."

The moment Claire and Pete were gone, Pekin said, "It's Lily Grayson. The ghost is Lily Grayson!"

"It has to be," Amber said. "Now we can talk to her."

"Well, it definitely helps," Scout said.

Claire joined them again. "I'm sorry about that. Pete's not as sharp as he used to be, I'm afraid. He struggles to remember anymore."

"You don't need to apologize for him," Amber said. "My grandma has dementia. I know he does his best, like my grandma does."

"It must be so hard," Pekin said.

"At times, yes," Claire said, "but he's still my Pete. He's a good man. Taking care of him now is such a small price to pay for the wonderful life he's given me. We were childhood sweethearts, you know. We married young and had children who now have successful lives of their own. I wouldn't trade a moment of my life with him. Even now." Her eyes grew misty.

"He's really lucky to have you," Scout said. "I mean, having someone love you so much is very special."

"Thank you, Scout. I'm lucky, too." She smiled. "So, is there anything else you all would like to hear about?"

"Yeah. I wonder about Mr. Grayson and the baby. So, they didn't stay long after his wife passed away?" Pekin asked.

"No. They were gone within a couple of months. Pete and I went over to help him out in any way we could. Took him dinners. That kind of thing. They didn't have family around, so I watched the baby for him while he had to work. She was a sweet little thing, and he was at a loss, so I was glad to help. I showed him how to diaper the baby, feed her, bathe her. Violet arrived before Lily and Ron had taken their infant care class." She sighed. "I've often wondered through the years what happened to her, to them."

She shook her head. "It was all a long time ago. The Dwyers are wonderful people, as you must surely know. I'm sure they'll have a measure of comfort knowing you three are looking after their things. And little Spike, of course."

"Yeah, Spike's fun. He's especially attached to Scout," Pekin said.

"He's my little buddy," Scout agreed.

Amber laughed. "He follows Scout around like a shadow."

"That's wonderful," Claire said. "Is there anything else I can help you with?"

"Thank you, but we should get out of your hair," Pekin said. "It was nice of you to invite us over."

"And feed us," Scout added with a smile.

"Well, it's been lovely meeting you all. Thank you so much for coming to lunch."

"We really enjoyed ourselves and appreciate your filling us in on the history of the Dwyers' house."

"Happy to help. If you need anything during your stay, please don't be afraid to call on me."

# Chapter Ten

ALL OF THEM WERE ANXIOUS to get back to the house and try to find Lily Grayson. They thought she might respond to her name, but after wandering through the upstairs rooms calling for her, it was with a sense of discouragement that the three of them gathered again in the family room. Scout flipped on the TV and absently searched through the guide for something to take their minds off how disappointed they all were.

Spike was curled up on the couch next to Scout, who'd nodded off, while Pekin and Amber had their noses buried in their phones. Nothing on TV had captured their interest as the afternoon drug on.

A sharp bark pulled Scout out of his snooze. He rubbed his eyes and stretched, but when Spike jumped off the couch and focused his attention on the stairs, all eyes turned to see what the little dog was looking at.

"Do you think—" Amber started.

"I think animals are more sensitive than humans are. Griselda always freaks when Miranda's around. I think Lily might be up there."

"Then let's go," Scout said, heading toward the stairwell.

They felt the chill before they reached the second floor. As they gathered on the landing, a ghostly form glided down the hallway, seemingly oblivious to their presence.

Amber gasped and put a hand over her mouth. "What do we do?" she whispered.

Pekin squared her shoulders and stepped in the ghost's path. If she'd hoped the ghost would acknowledge her and stop, she was wrong. The spirit passed right through her. Pekin shuddered and rubbed her hands up and down her arms.

Scout was immediately at her side. "Are you all right?"

Pekin nodded, her eyes big. "It feels really weird when that happens. I'm freezing."

He took her hands. "Wow, you *are* cold."

"Where did she go?" Amber asked.

"I think she went in the master bedroom," Scout said.

"Let's go then," Pekin said.

Of course, when they got there, no ghost was in sight.

"Lily," Pekin called out. "Lily, we're here to help you. We want to talk to you. Can you come out?"

"We know what happened to you," Amber said. "It's so sad. We know about Violet."

Pekin froze, unsure how the ghost would respond to hearing her daughter's name. But the room was warm, and no spirit appeared, angry or otherwise.

"She's gone," Pekin said. "We might as well go back downstairs."

Reluctantly, the three of them left the bedroom. At the

landing, Pekin looked over her shoulder at the master bedroom, before following Scout and Amber.

No sooner had they reached the bottom step when they heard a sob. As quietly as they could, they rushed back up the stairs. All three heads whipped toward the bedroom as more sobs floated on the air. Pekin put a finger to her lips and tiptoed toward the open door of the master bedroom. She could hear the soft footsteps of her friends behind her. The chill was already spreading out into the hallway causing the kids to shiver.

The spirit sat on the bed, her face buried in her hands, the sound of the ghostly sobs casting an eerie pall in the room.

"Say something." Amber poked Pekin in the side.

"Shush!" Pekin said. She looked at Scout, lifting her shoulders in a *what should I do?* motion.

He nodded toward the ghost, mouthing, "Go for it."

"Lily?" Pekin said tentatively. "Lily? Can you hear me?" She watched the ghost, who kept sobbing.

"I don't think she hears me," Pekin said.

"Try again," Scout said.

"Lily!" Pekin said, more sharply than she intended.

The ghost's head jerked up and it looked toward Pekin, who gulped and took a step back. The ghost was motionless, just watching her.

Pekin cleared her throat. "Lily?" she said nervously.

The ghost rose from the bed, still not taking its eyes off Pekin, and drifted toward her.

"Scout?" Pekin whimpered. He stepped up and took her hand.

"I'm here."

The ghost, who was taller than Pekin, moved within a foot of her face, glaring down at her.

"Lily?" Pekin said again. "We just want to talk to you—"

*Where's my baby?* the ghost screeched.

Pekin backed up into Scout's arms and hid her face for a moment. She could tell by the chill that the ghost was still there.

"Your baby is all grown up now. She's okay, Lily." Pekin looked up into the angry transparent face.

*Where's my baby?* The ghost waved its arms in the air, and Pekin squeaked as Scout pulled her backward out of the room. He handed her off to Amber then faced the ghost and waved his arms back at her.

"Leave her alone. She doesn't have your baby. If you want us to help you, you can't go around scaring people like that. Pekin only wants to talk to you."

The ghost vanished, and the room grew warm again.

Pekin pulled away from Amber and flew down the stairs, followed by her friends. Spike was hopping up and down barking at the bottom of the stairs and wound around their legs as they rushed back to the family room and collapsed on the couch. Scout sat beside Pekin and put a protective arm around her shoulders.

She took a couple of deep breaths, then smiled. "That was amazing!"

"Are you okay?" Amber asked, confused. "I thought you were scared."

"I wasn't—"

"You were," Scout said. "Admit it."

"Okay, I was scared. But she didn't hurt me or anything."

"Not yet."

"I'm not sure I want to sleep in that room tonight," Amber said. "I'm going to stay down here tonight."

"You're abandoning me?" Pekin asked in alarm.

"You can sleep in that scary room if you want to but count me out. If that ghost could scare *you*, I for sure don't want to come face to face with it."

"But Scout can stay with us," Pekin said.

"Or," Amber countered, "Scout *and* you can bring your pillows and blankets down here and we can all sleep in front of the TV. Where it's safe."

"Maybe Amber's right," Scout said. "Just for tonight, we should all stick together."

Turned out the couch was a sleeper and, when unfolded, was big enough for both Pekin and Amber to sleep on. Scout discovered that the recliner opened almost flat, was comfortable, and spared him having to spend a second night on the floor.

"Too bad we didn't think of this last night," he said as he settled into the cushy recliner, squirming around to find the most comfortable position.

"This does seem kind of cozy," Amber said. "But, I have to say, it will be good when this week is over and I can sleep fear-free in my own bed."

"It hasn't been that scary," Pekin said, with a scowl. "I'm the one the ghost walked through. It's not like she tried to hurt me."

"Well, she did get kind of threatening, yelling and waving aggressively," Scout said.

"Oh, yeah," Pekin said. "There was that."

"Anyway," Scout said, "I'm sure we're safe here. So, sleep tight, Amber."

"What about me?" Pekin asked.

"Yeah. You, too, Pekie."

Spike curled up in Scout's lap for the night and didn't wake up barking even once to announce a ghostly visitor.

# Chapter Eleven

"**B**ENNY'S AGAIN?" AMBER ASKED as she sat up and yawned. Pekin rubbed her eyes and Scout stretched his arms above his head.

"Oh, yeah," he said.

"We're spending a lot of money at Benny's," Pekin said. "Should we stop and pick up cereal and milk after breakfast? You know, to cut down on our expenses?"

"And peanut butter," Amber added. "We can make our own lunches."

"Then let's get dressed and get out of here," Pekin said. "I'm starving."

Pekin's phone dinged on the way into the diner and, once they were seated, she pulled up the text.

"It's from my mom," she said, scanning the screen. "She said Miranda popped in on her."

"Really? I miss her," Amber said.

"Well, Mom says she might be popping in on us. She was looking for me when she visited my mom."

The server arrived, poised to take their orders. He shook his head and laughed. "Let me guess. The usual?" The

Ghosties laughed back.

"Why mess with success?" Scout said with a grin.

After the server left with their orders, Pekin said, "Mom said she looks different. Can't wait to see what she meant."

# Chapter Twelve

~~~~~~~~~~~~~~~~~~~~~~~~~~~~~~~~~~~~~~~~~~~~~~~~~~~~~~~~~~~~~~

WHAT PEKIN'S MOM MEANT was that Miranda had changed clothes. Their ghostly friend popped in on them at Firefly Lane shortly after they returned from the market. Instead of wearing a pretty, frilly dress with ribbons and Mary Janes, Miranda was wearing a peasant blouse over linen draw-string pants, and sandals.

"Miranda!" Pekin said, frowning at the barking dog who had plastered himself to Scout's leg. "It's okay, Spike. Miranda's a friend."

That assurance didn't register with Spike, who growled under his breath between barks.

"Scout, can you do something about that?" Pekin asked.

Scout gathered the little dog in his arms and cooed softly to him, an action which, again, didn't register with Spike. Scout finally shoved Spike into a sitting position behind his back on the couch, which seemed to do the trick as the barking trailed off and Spike contented himself with peeking around Scout and growling quietly.

"Thanks," Pekin said, before turning to Miranda. "How did you do that?"

"Yeah," Amber said. "How did you change your clothes?"

*I've been practicing.*

"So, how did you decide what to wear?" Amber said.

*It was in a window, so I thought it and it became.*

"Well, you look adorable," Pekin said.

*Does it look okay?* the ghost asked.

"Um, yeah," Amber said hesitantly. She seemed like she wouldn't say any more, but then added, "It's kind of old for you. Not like a kid would wear."

Miranda looked downcast and Amber immediately regretted her words.

"Do you want us to help you pick stuff out?" Pekin asked.

Miranda closed her eyes tightly and squeezed her fists. The air shimmered and suddenly the ghost had on shorts and an orange Cheshire cat T-shirt. An outfit identical to Pekin's. And her blonde curls were now pulled back in a ponytail.

Pekin looked at Miranda, then down at herself. "Um—"

"You look very nice, Miranda," Scout said.

A blush crept up Miranda's transparent cheeks and she smiled.

"You have a Mini-Me, Pekie," Scout said.

Pekin scrutinized Miranda. "You got all the details right," she said. "You even have the same tennis shoes and hairdo."

"I thought you didn't have hairdos," Scout said with a smirk.

"Oh, shut up," Pekin said, giving him a shove. "Lucky for Miranda you can't mess up her hair like you do mine."

He laughed.

"So, really, how does that work?" Pekin asked Miranda. "I didn't know you could change clothes like that."

*I'm not sure. But no one looks like I do. I wanted to be like everyone else, so I started trying to will it into being. After a lot of practicing, it worked.*

"Wish I had that magic power," Amber said. "Then I could have fabulous outfits all the time."

"You have great clothes," Pekin said.

"Then why did Miranda copy you and not me?" Amber looked comical, standing with her nose in the air and her hands on her hips in pretend displeasure, and Pekin laughed.

"I don't know. Why don't you ask her?"

Miranda looked stricken, her hand covering her mouth and her eyes big.

"Oh, no, Miranda. I was just kidding. I didn't really mean it," Amber said, looking for someone to help her convince the ghost that she hadn't done anything wrong.

"She always kids like that," Pekin said. "You can dress like anyone you want to and we won't tease you anymore."

"So, do you want to hear about our case?" Scout asked Miranda. "Maybe you can help."

Miranda looked at him gratefully and plopped down on the floor to listen.

"A ghost named Lily lives here. Or, you know, maybe not *lives*. Anyway, she died in childbirth and now she's looking for her baby," Amber said. "The Dwyers...they're the ones who called us...they like her and call her Windy because it's always cold when she's around. Beside the point, sorry. We tried to get the ghost to talk to us and it got very agitated and kind of scared Pekin. So now we have to figure out what to do next."

She grabbed her phone off the coffee table. "I think we should do an internet search for Violet. If she's on there, maybe we can contact her and see if she'll come back and give her mother peace."

"Not a bad idea," Scout said. "We could look for her dad, first, though. If Violet has gotten married, then her name could be different."

"Violet is Lily's daughter and is a grown up now," Amber said to Miranda.

"Hey, can ghosts find other ghosts?" Pekin asked Miranda. "Like, could you go upstairs and Lily would know you were there and come out and talk to you?"

*No. Probably not. Lily would be on another plane, not waiting up there.*

"Really? There's another plane? Is that what you did?" Amber asked.

*It was safer for me there. Then George couldn't get me.*

"Why didn't you stay on that plane, then?" Scout asked.

*It's a nothing. I mean, there's nothing to do there. No one else is there. It's a place to rest. I would miss my home. I didn't like the other plane.*

"So, George wasn't on the other plane with you?" Pekin asked.

*No. It's not just a big space with lots of spirits around. It's personal to each of us. Like a time out.*

"Grrrr," came a rumble from the little dog.

"What was Lily's husband's name?" Amber asked, pulling her laptop out of her backpack, deciding it was easier to navigate on than her phone.

"I think it's Ron," Scout said.

"He's right," Pekin said. "I made a point of remembering when Claire told us."

"So, okay. Ron Grayson." She was already typing the name in the search field. "Wow. There are a ton of them."

Pekin peered over Amber's shoulder, as her friend scanned through the list of Ron Graysons. Most of them were easy to discard, but there were four that were potential.

From the pictures, each looked to be in the right age range for someone who had been a young father in 1997. The first of those was located in Maine. So, unlikely.

The second was in Denver. That left two, both of whom were in Louisiana, where Ron Grayson had moved with his daughter. Amber sent a friend request to both of them, hoping her location in Springdale might spark some interest.

"It's so weird you have a Facebook account," Pekin said. "Since mostly old people use that."

"Don't tease me," Amber said. "I set it up a few years ago to share pictures with my grandparents. Just my family and you guys are my friends on it."

"Yeah," Scout said. "Don't tease Amber. Remember, Ron's old so this might be the best way to reach him."

"I was only kidding anyway," Pekin said. "Scout's right. Maybe it will help us."

Next, Amber searched for Violet Grayson. None of the responses seemed to be the person they were looking for, either by age or location, although the kids realized that she could have moved, for college or marriage or some other reason.

Now, their hopes were pinned on Ron Grayson's friend request.

"Hey, we knew it was a longshot that we'd get an answer just like that," Scout said.

"I know, but what do we do now?" Pekin asked.

"We wait, I guess, and try communicating with Lily again."

Miranda took in all the disappointed faces. *Is this what it was like...with me?*

"Kind of," Pekin said. "It took a couple of days before we saw any sign of you. Then, when we did, we had to get you to trust us. So, yes, it was frustrating at the beginning."

*I'm sorry*, the ghost said.

"You don't have to be sorry. Why should you have automatically wanted anything to do with us in the beginning? We were strangers. You had no reason to trust us."

"Pekin's right. And, don't forget, you were a success story. So you have nothing to apologize for," Scout said.

"Man, it feels like we've been at this for hours, and it's not even lunchtime yet," Amber said.

"I wish we had Claire Masterson's phone number," Pekin said.

All eyes turned her way.

"We didn't think to ask if Ron left her a forwarding address or anything. If he did, it would be a place to start."

"You're right," Scout said. "Should we go over there and see if they're home?"

"I vote yes," Amber said.

"Let's go then," Pekin said.

"Maybe just you should go," Scout said. "Less disruptive that way. We don't want them to think they have to invite us in and entertain us."

"But——"

"I mean, we can go, too, if you need us to," he said.

Pekin shrugged. "No. I'll just hop over there. Hopefully, I'll be back in ten minutes."

It was actually closer to fifteen minutes before Pekin was back with her friends. "It was embarrassing," she said. "She seemed confused that I was asking about that. I had to come up with a reason off the top of my head. So I told her we were making a house tree."

"Huh?" Amber said.

"You know. A house tree. Like a family tree. Give me a break. I had to think fast."

"The only problem with that is Claire might ask Edie about the house tree after they get back."

Pekin waved Scout off. "I can't be bothered with that right now."

"So, did you get it?" Amber asked.

"Yeah. Claire has a really old address book. She flipped it open and found it right away. Seems weird writing down all those contacts like that."

"They didn't have cell phones back then," Scout said dryly.

"I suppose. Anyway, here it is." Pekin handed over the slip of note paper with the address and phone number on it.

"I don't suppose that number is still good?" Amber said.

"I doubt it. No cell phones, remember?" Scout said. "And most people don't have a landline anymore."

"So, what does it say?" Amber asked.

"It's an address in Metairie. Wasn't one of those Ron Graysons in Metairie?" Scout said.

"Yeah. Sounds like he's the most promising of the Facebook people. Let's Google Map it," Pekin said. "Use the satellite view."

Amber typed in the address and used the zoom feature to go to street level. Her heart sank. "It doesn't look like anyone lives there anymore." She turned the laptop so everyone else could see it. The house had definitely fallen into disrepair, but so had the rest of the neighborhood. "It looks deserted."

"In other words, a dead end," Pekin said.

"Not necessarily," Scout said. "Just a hiccup."

"If only we could go there and search around, like real detectives."

"Yeah. I don't think we could get our parents to spring for airfare and lodging," Amber said. "And that's if we could even convince them to let us go."

"How long would it take to drive there?" Pekin asked.

"Oh, right. It's only like a thousand miles or so," Scout said. "The Dwyers would be back from their cruise before we even got there."

"Maybe we could send Mildew," Pekin said.

"Or maybe we should wait to see if we hear from one of the Rons," Scout said.

*I could go there,* Miranda said, *but I don't know what to do.*

"That's sweet of you," Pekin said. "But I don't even know what *we'd* do if we managed to get there." She dropped her head and sighed. "Dang it."

"What are we going to say if Ron confirms our friend request?" Amber asked.

"I guess if he confirms us, we can search his Facebook page for Violet. You'd think she'd be active on his page," Pekin said.

Spike, who'd been cowering behind Scout all this time, stuck his head out and gave a brave bark before darting back.

Pekin closed her eyes and shook her head.

# CHAPTER THIRTEEN

"SHOULD WE CHECK OUT THE ATTIC?" Amber asked. "In case there might be clues?"

"I guess we could, while we're waiting on Ron," Scout said.

"Or," Pekin said, "Miranda could go up there to see if there's even anything up there."

"Would you want to do that, Miranda?" Amber asked.

*I will if you like*, the ghost said.

"Come on. We'll show you where it is," Scout said.

Three kids, with Miranda floating after them, tromped up the stairs and stood underneath the oblong panel in the ceiling.

"Will you be able to see up there if there's no light?" Amber asked Miranda.

*I don't need light*, came the reply, right before the ghost disappeared.

The kids waited in the hallway below, all eyes on the ceiling, until Miranda reappeared.

*There are a handful of boxes, not a lot. Some old clothes. And a cradle.*

"A cradle! That could be Violet's baby bed," Amber said.

"But wouldn't Ron have taken that with them when he moved away?" Pekin asked.

"Maybe, or maybe he needed something bigger. He must have stayed here for several weeks, since Claire said she babysat for him. Violet would have grown out of it quickly and he probably didn't want to cart it with him since the baby could only use it for a short time," Scout said.

"We could bring it down," Amber said.

"I don't know," Pekin said. "What if it freaked Lily out? There wouldn't be a baby in it and it might make things even worse."

"I hadn't thought of that," Amber said.

"So, what do we do now?" Pekin asked.

"If Lily doesn't show up, there's not a lot we *can* do," Scout said. "Let's go downstairs. With any luck, Ron will confirm our friend request. Then we'll have a path forward."

It was a trudge downstairs for the three kids. Not one of them had a better idea.

"WHAT HAVE YOU BEEN DOING since the last time we saw you?" Amber asked Miranda.

*I went to my school. It's very different now. I spent time at the cemetery. I sat at my parents' graves, and mine. It was odd. And some of the time I was in the place I can go when I want to be alone.*

"The other plane you told us about?" Pekin said.

*Yes. When I feel overwhelmed by how different everything is, I go there.*

Amber's phone dinged. "Ron Grayson confirmed our friend request."

"Let's go," Scout said. "Pull it up."

Amber flipped open her laptop and accessed her Facebook page.

She clicked on Ron Grayson's name and was taken to his page. On the left side were pictures of friends. In the center were Ron's posts, which Amber scanned. It took a moment of scanning, but the name "Violet" sprang out at them.

"There!" Pekin pointed to the post, which was a "Happy Birthday to my wonderful daughter" message, with congratulatory responses. There were also thank-you messages from a Violet Sparks.

Before anyone could say "go there," Amber had already clicked on Violet's link and immediately submitted a friend request. With Pekin and Scout crowded around her, she slowly moved down Violet's posts. It appeared that Violet had a daughter. A little blonde toddler with curly pigtails was laughing and splashing in a backyard wading pool, her chubby arms waving in the air.

"Aww, she's so *cute*," Amber gushed. "Have you ever seen anything so adorable?"

"She is cute," Pekin agreed. "But we're looking for clues. Can you find anything that shows where they're located?"

"Or do you see anything about her husband?"

"Let me look," Amber said, continuing to scan the posts. "Here's someone saying she bets David will love that."

"Love what?" Pekin asked.

"I don't know. But it sounds like it could be referring to

a significant other. Let's see if we can find a Violet or David Sparks on Google."

Amber googled David Sparks and silently scanned the links that appeared, with Pekin and Scout still peering over her shoulder.

Without warning, and almost bumping her head on Pekin's chin, Amber sat up straight. "Oh, my God. You guys, look at this. David Sparks works at the medical center in Yardley. Yardley's only an hour and a half from here!"

"An hour and a half," Pekin mused.

"Do you know what that means?" Amber asked, her eyes shining.

"We can go talk to him," Pekin said.

"Right. We can ask him about Violet."

Amber's nose was buried in her computer again. A Facebook notification popped up and, eyes never leaving the screen, she said Ron sent her a PM.

"What does it say?" Pekin asked.

"He's asking if we're...I'm... from Springdale. And he asked if he knows me. What should I say?"

"Tell him you're friends with the Mastersons, and ask if he remembers them."

Amber typed quickly, then looked up at her friends. Everyone held their breath as they waited for a reply.

It didn't take long before the laptop dinged and launched Amber into action. "He says he remembers them. He wants to know how they are."

"Tell him you heard all about him and Violet from the Mastersons. Tell him we'd love to meet Violet. See if you can get him to tell you where she is."

"That's kind of creepy," Scout said. "In a stalkery kind of way, isn't it?"

"I got this," Amber said and started to type, pausing to think about how to phrase it, then started typing again.

"I said they're good. I asked if he and Violet still live around here."

The waiting was a nightmare. Scout was pacing, Pekin was tapping her foot, and Amber kept her eyes glued to the screen.

Ding.

"He says he's in Louisiana, and that Violet lives outside Yardley with her husband and daughter."

Amber started typing again. "I told him it was nice connecting with him and thanked him for accepting my friend request." She closed her laptop.

"I didn't want to chat all day," she said.

"He confirmed that Violet's in the Yardley area. Maybe we can find her," Pekin said.

# Chapter Fourteen

~~~~~~~~~~~~~~~~~~~~~~~~~~~~~~~~~~~~~~~~~~~~~~~~~~~~~~~

FURIOUS BARKING SOUNDED from behind Scout's back and Spike's head appeared. He wasn't looking in Miranda's direction, but toward the stairs.

Scout tucked Spike under his arm and all of them headed for the stairs. Before Scout took the first step, however, Spike managed to wiggle out of his arm and scamper from the room, his little feet skittering on the wood floor.

Scout watched him go, then turned to his friends. "Let's go."

The second floor felt twenty degrees colder than the lower level, and Pekin rubbed her arms and shivered. They all saw the shimmer in the hallway at the same time as the ghostly form glided toward the master bedroom.

"What do we do?" whispered Amber, her eyes big.

"Pekin, you stay back," Scout said. "We don't need her to attack you again."

*What about me?* Miranda asked.

The kids looked at her and watched as she moved into the hallway into the path of the oncoming spirit.

*Lily?* Miranda tried. The other ghost pulled up short and screeched. Then disappeared.

"No!" Pekin cried. "Lily, come back!"

Lily's spirit didn't reappear, not that they expected her to.

"What happened?" Amber asked.

"I guess she wasn't happy another ghost was in her house," Scout said.

"What do you think?" Pekin asked Miranda.

*I felt anger from her. I'm sorry.*

"Don't be sorry. None of us knows what to do. At least you tried," Scout said.

A whoosh of cold air in the hallway ripped a picture from the wall causing it to crash to the floor, the glass shattering. Freezing wind swirled around the three kids, pushing them back toward the stairway.

"I guess she really *is* mad," Amber said. "Let's get out of here." She turned and rushed down the stairs, followed by Scout. Before Pekin could follow, the wind knocked her down and spun her around and she skidded down the hall toward the back of the house.

"Help me," she screamed, cowering as the angry spirit hovered over her, trying to pull her hair.

Scout ran toward Pekin, but Lily whirled and waved her arm. A force flung him backward, and only Amber rushing behind him kept him from smacking his head on the hardwood floor as she blocked his fall.

Lily turned back toward Pekin, her hands grasping at the petrified girl.

Scout clambered to his feet and ran to Pekin. By the time he got her off the floor, she was in tears. "She wants to hurt me!" she said through chattering teeth.

"Get away from her!" Scout bellowed at Lily. He positioned himself between Pekin and the ghost and rushed his girlfriend down the stairs. Thankfully, the spirit didn't follow.

He pulled Pekin into his arms, letting her sob, her shoulders shaking, as he smoothed her hair. When she was in control of herself, he sat her down on the couch and took her hands. "Are you all right?"

She sniffled and nodded. She tried to speak, but nerves got the better of her and it took a moment before she could answer. "I could feel her fingers poking into me, like icicles. I still feel the cold to my core. I didn't know what she might do to me."

"That was *so* scary," Amber said, looking up at the second floor.

"We should always stay together when we go up there," Scout said. "You hear me, Pekie?"

"It wasn't my fault. It got me before I could follow you."

"I know. We all need to be more careful, though."

A loud wailing came from upstairs followed by a cry of *I want my baby*. The sound of wind howling through the rooms and knocking things off tables and dressers causing the kids to cringe.

"Oh, my God," Amber said. "She's destroying the Dwyers' house! We have to do something."

Pekin wiped her eyes and took a deep breath, then

rushed up the stairs before anyone could stop her. She heard Scout yell "Pekin" after her.

The sound of breaking glass came from the master bedroom and she flew toward the sound.

The ghost's eyes were sweeping the room, searching desperately. Pekin came to a stop just inside the door. She gulped and took another step into the room, fighting the panic that threatened to cause her to turn and run.

"Lily. Listen to me. We're here to find your baby." The swirling wind didn't lessen, so Pekin shouted. "Lily! We're going to find your baby and bring her home to you. We're going to find Violet! Please stop."

The wind died down, but the chill remained. "Thank you, Lily. We know what happened to you and that you have a daughter named Violet. You chose that name. It's a beautiful name. Please trust us. We already know what city she's in. We'll do our best to bring her back to you." The ghost had spun to face Pekin, her face unreadable.

Scout and Amber, who'd rushed upstairs at Pekin's shouting, tumbled in the bedroom doorway.

"What the *heck*, Pekie. Are you okay?" Scout asked, taking her arm and pulling her around to face him.

"Why did you do that?" Amber hissed, her eyes wide. "She could have hurt you."

"I think she listened," Pekin said. When she looked back to where the spirit had stood, it was gone, and the temperature in the room had returned to normal.

Miranda hovered in the doorway. *The angry energy is gone.*

"Where were you, Miranda?" Pekin asked.

*I…was afraid.*

"You were afraid it might be like George?" Amber asked.

The ghost looked down and nodded.

"It's okay, Miranda," Amber said. "We understand."

"I guess we should see what she damaged," Scout said.

"You mean destroyed?" Amber grumbled. "I heard a lot of glass breaking."

A small vase in the master bedroom lay in pieces on the floor. "That was a pretty vase," Amber said. "The Dwyers are going to hate us."

"Shaking things up was bound to agitate the ghost," Scout said. "All Lily knows is that we're intruding. With any luck, Pekin got through to her."

"I hope so," Pekin said. "Now all we have to do is actually find Violet and convince her to come back here." She tapped her finger on her lips. "I want to go talk to Claire Masterson again."

"Huh?" Scout said, tilting his head.

"That cradle, the one Miranda found in the attic. If it was for Violet, maybe she'd like to have it, as a memento of her mother. I want to ask Claire what she knows about it."

"That's a great idea," Amber said.

"Can we call her instead of dropping in again?" Scout asked.

"Let's see if we can find her number," Pekin said.

Next to the wall phone in the kitchen, Pekin found an address book.

"This is like an antique," she said. "Can you imagine having to write down phone numbers in a book?"

"No kidding. What a pain." Amber sent an adoring glance to her iPhone. "Did you find a number?"

"Yeah. I guess we're lucky Edie has one of those antiques. Claire's number is right here under 'M.'"

Pekin drew in her breath and dialed, looking around at her friends as the phone rang on the other end.

Claire remembered the cradle well. She'd visited with Lily as the mother-to-be painted the baby bed, which had been passed down to Lily from her own mother. "Ron sanded off the old varnish and Lily painted it white, then added bunches of peonies tied with ribbons. Painted them, I mean," she said. "It was a pretty little thing."

"Why wouldn't Ron have taken it with him?" Pekin asked.

"Violet outgrew it? By the time they moved away, it might have been getting too small. I don't know if he forgot about it or left it because it reminded him too much of Lily."

Pekin thanked her for the information and turned, smiling, to Amber and Scout. "It was hand-painted by Lily, after she inherited it from her own mother. I bet Violet would *love* to have it. Maybe that's a way we can get her to come here."

"Um, I don't think we can just break into the Dwyers' attic and give it away. It doesn't belong to us," Scout said.

Pekin frowned. "Well, we can at least show it to her. Then, if she wants it, we can try to convince the Dwyers to give it to her. I mean, they hired us to help Lily, and that would be helping her. Don't you think Lily would be happy to know her daughter had the cradle she'd labored over?"

"Maybe. Probably. But, before we do anything else, we should go back upstairs and see what else Lily destroyed," Scout said.

"Oh, yeah. That," Amber said. "I'm afraid to look."

Pekin frowned, and turned toward the stairs. "Come on. Let's get this over with."

It turned out the damage was minimal. A couple of picture frames were on the floor, the glass shattered. Books littered the floor in a guest bedroom with a small bookcase. Pillows tossed off beds. Crooked paintings on the walls.

The cleanup was quick. Books were re-shelved and paintings straightened. Scout promised to replace the glass in the frames, leaving the only real damage the broken blue vase.

"I hope it wasn't an antique," Amber said. "An irreplaceable family heirloom."

"Me, too," Pekin said.

# Chapter Fifteen

"I DON'T KNOW ABOUT YOU GUYS, but I'm hungry," Scout said, heading down the stairs and flopping on the couch in the family room. "Can we make sandwiches?"

"I found peanut butter and jelly," Pekin called from the kitchen. "I'll make some."

Amber sat beside Scout and flipped open her laptop. "I have a PM from Ron," she said.

Scout scooted closer so he could see the screen.

*I'd appreciate it if you didn't contact my daughter. The past is the past, and it should stay there. I hope you understand.*

"What's *that* all about?" Scout asked.

"What happened?" Pekin stuck her head out of the kitchen.

"Ron Grayson sent a message to Amber to stay away from his daughter. I think he's unfriending us."

"Why wouldn't he want us to talk to Violet?"

"Let me ask him," Amber said, typing a short response. "I said I don't understand and that we weren't trying to interfere or anything. I asked why he doesn't want us to contact his daughter."

"I don't think he's going to respond," Scout said. "The message he sent was kind of a kiss off."

"That leaves us with contacting her husband?" Amber said.

*I could follow the thread,* Miranda said. All three teens looked at her.

"What thread?" Pekin asked.

*There's a silver thread connecting people who belong to each other. Like a daughter belongs to her mother. In a way.*

"Did you have a silver thread?" Amber asked, her eyes wide.

*There was no one for a thread to connect to. Everyone I loved was already gone.*

"So, the thread is only to a living person?" Scout asked.

*Yes.*

"Is it like a cable running down the middle of the street?" Pekin asked.

*No. Not really. It's thin and ethereal.*

"And you can follow it?"

*Yes.*

"Can you take us there?" Amber said.

*No. The thread doesn't go in a straight line. I can follow it but not with you.*

Amber looked disappointed.

*But I can go where it leads and then take you there.*

"That's amazing," Pekin said, a smile growing on her face. "Miranda, you may have saved the day."

The ghost smiled shyly. *Shall I go now?*

"If you don't mind," Pekin said, at the same time Amber said, "Yes!"

"Sorry," Amber said. "I just can't wait."

Miranda disappeared, leaving Pekin, Scout and Amber to stare at the empty place she'd stood only moments before.

"I'm nervous," Pekin said. Scout took her hand and squeezed it, then slipped his arm around her. She glowed as she looked up at him.

"Thanks," she said shyly, then impulsively put her arms around him, resting her face against his shoulder. He ruffled her hair, which, thankfully, was hanging loose and not in a ponytail he could mess up.

Pekin laughed and let him go. "I have to go finish the sandwiches."

The teens ate mostly in silence, everyone's thoughts on what Miranda would discover.

Afterward, sitting in the family room, the wait continued for what seemed an endless amount of time until a shimmer appeared in their midst.

"Miranda!" Amber said. "Did you find her?"

*She was in her home.*

"Where does she live?" Pekin asked.

"What's she like?" Amber interrupted excitedly.

*I memorized her house number*, the ghost said. *She lives at 2339 Orchard Street. I believe the town is Yardley.*

"What was she doing when you saw her?" Pekin asked.

*She was in the kitchen, preparing food.*

"Is she pretty?" Amber asked. "Does she look happy?"

*She seemed content.*

"Well, when can we go there?" Amber asked.

"Yardley is more than an hour away. It's getting toward

late afternoon. Maybe we should go tomorrow morning?" Scout said.

"Miranda, would you be able to go back tomorrow morning and check if she's home, so we know where to find her?" Pekin asked.

*If it will help.*

# Chapter Sixteen

M IRANDA SHOWED UP the next morning while the kids were having cereal. Actually, a shimmer appeared and then vanished. A second later, the full Miranda showed up wearing jeans shorts, a pink lace crop top and flip flops, an exact replica of the outfit Amber was wearing, right down to the pink headband holding her hair back.

"Miranda copied *me* this morning." Amber's grin was huge. "Thanks, Miranda!"

The ghost ducked her head and shyly smiled up at Amber. *I liked it.*

Miranda was becoming more solid. Not nearly as see-through as she'd appeared when they first met her. The ghost kid was picking up things. She was barely transparent now.

"So, you guys ready to go?" Pekin asked as each of them rinsed out their cereal bowl and loaded it into the dishwasher. "Miranda, can you zoom over there and see if she's home before we set off on an hour-long trip?"

"Sure," Miranda said, disappearing.

"How long do you think it will take her?" Amber asked.

"I don't know. This is new to us."

"She's baa-ack," Scout said in a sing-song voice.

*Violet is in her house, doing housework*, Miranda reported.

"I guess it's a go then," Pekin said, grabbing up her backpack and heading for the front door.

The four of them piled into Scout's Corolla and set off for Yardley.

It was a beautiful drive, through countryside and woods, but everyone's focus was on meeting Violet Sparks and figuring out how to convince her to come back to Springdale to meet her mother's ghost.

Not your usual conversation.

Violet's home was a beautifully maintained sprawling ranch-style in an upscale neighborhood. It was painted a fashionable gray with blue trim. The front featured full-size windows across the front of the house.

"Oh, she'll see us coming up the walk," Amber said with a frown.

"She probably sees lots of people coming up her walk. I doubt we'll freak her out," Pekin said.

"Until we tell her why we're here," Scout said.

"Speaking of that," Pekin said. "Should we go up there?"

"I'm scared," Amber said.

Pekin rolled her eyes. "That's *so* you, Amber."

"Well, what are we going to say to her?" Amber asked.

"I don't know. We'll see how it goes."

"That gives me a lot of confidence," Amber said, climbing out of the car.

They all looked at each other for courage and followed Pekin up to the front door.

She rang the bell then stood back, her sweaty hands folded in front of her. Footsteps could be heard approaching and the door swung open.

"Um, may I help you?" the pretty woman who answered the door asked, a suspicious look on her face, which made sense given that usually when teenagers showed up at her door it was to try and sell her something.

"Hi, Ms. Sparks?" Pekin asked. When the woman nodded, Pekin continued. "My name is Pekin Dewlap and these are my friends Scout and Amber and…"

She started to say "and Miranda," but realized the mistake in time to stop herself.

"And…can I help you?"

"Sorry. We're Facebook friends of your father."

Violet's face changed from suspicious to confused when the kids mentioned being Facebook friends with a man who was probably older than their parents.

"And, um, we're from your hometown, Springdale."

"My hometown isn't Springdale," Violet said. "I think you must be mistaken."

"No, I mean, you were born in Springdale, but your dad moved you away when you were a baby."

"Not that I know of," she responded.

Pekin looked at Scout and Amber, panicked.

"We wanted to talk to you about your mother," Scout said.

"What do you know about Andrea?"

Now the kids were confused. "Andrea? No. Lily. Your mother, Lily."

"My mother's name was Andrea. I'm sorry, but I think you have the wrong person."

"But—" Pekin started but was cut off by the door, which closed before she could finish saying whatever it was that might have come out of her mouth. Pekin herself didn't know how she would have completed the thought.

"Well, *that* went well," Scout said as they trailed back to the car.

"What's going on?" Pekin said. "We know she's the right person."

"Do we?" Amber asked. "Maybe we didn't look hard enough."

"No, we did. Her dad remembered the Mastersons."

Pekin tapped her lips thoughtfully with her finger. "And, don't forget, Miranda saw the silver thread."

"I did forget for a minute. I guess she really is Lily's daughter."

"So, what do we do now?" Scout asked.

Pekin slumped down in the front passenger seat. "I don't have a clue."

# Chapter Seventeen

〰〰〰〰〰〰〰〰〰〰〰〰〰〰〰〰〰〰〰〰〰〰〰

N O ONE SPOKE MUCH on the drive home. Miranda looked worriedly from one friend to another before finally sitting quietly mimicking her friends.

"I have an idea," Pekin announced as Scout parked in front of Firefly Lane.

She scrambled out of the car.

Scout and Amber joined her on the front walk. "Don't just stand there!" Amber said. "Tell us."

Pekin looked back over her shoulder as she unlocked the front door and stepped inside. "It's just an idea. I don't know if it will work." She paused. "And I don't think you're going to like it."

"I don't like it already, then," Scout said with a scowl. "You may as well go ahead and tell us."

"I was just wondering if maybe I could, um, communicate with Lily."

"Communicate how?" he asked.

"Like, maybe, I could open my mind and she could come in."

"What? Are you out of your mind?" Scout was livid.

"She's already made it clear she isn't happy with our presence. Wasn't having George take over your head enough?"

"Calm down," she said, placing her hand on his arm. "I mean, we could check with Mildew first and she could help, or she could think it's a terrible idea."

Pekin looked at the glum faces watching her. The tension in the air was unmistakable. "Come on, you guys," she pleaded. "We have to do *something*."

Amber threw up her hands and stomped out of the room. She was slipping her phone back in her pocket when she came back into the family room a minute later. "She'll be right here."

"Who?" Pekin asked.

"Mildew. She's freaked out, too."

"Really? You called her already?" Pekin crossed her arms over her chest and glared at Amber. "It was just an idea."

"And it was just an idea for you to go Elmwood in the middle of the night as well, and then you did it." Scout glared back. "Look how well that turned out."

Pekin tsked and shook her head. "You guys worry too much."

"And, apparently, you don't worry enough," Scout said. "I swear, Pekin, you're going to be the death of me."

"As long as you promise to haunt me when you're gone," she responded with a sheepish smile.

It was Scout's turn to shake his head in exasperation. Obviously, not amused.

"I'm going for a walk," he said. "Come on, Spike." He patted his leg and knelt to calm down the little dog who was bouncing up and down like a kangaroo before snapping on the leash and slamming the front door behind him.

"I think he's a little upset with you," Amber said.

"More than a little."

"Are you sure—"

"I'm not sure about anything. But this could work. If we could get Lily to be more like Miranda... I don't know. Maybe we could reason with her."

"Why do we need to reason with her?"

"Because. For one thing, even if Violet comes back here, she's not a baby anymore. What if Lily doesn't recognize her?"

"Good point. I didn't think of that."

Pekin headed for the kitchen, pulling a bottle of water out of the refrigerator. She handed one to Amber, then sat on a bar stool staring into space, sipping her water.

"I don't know, Pekin," Amber said, tossing her empty bottle into recycle. "I'm worried about Scout. He's not taking it well that you want to take such a big risk. He's afraid something will happen to you."

"Should I go after him?" Pekin asked, casting a worried glance toward the door.

"Probably. He's concerned about you, that's all."

Pekin unexpectedly hugged her friend. "Amber, I'm so lucky to have you as my best friend. You know I love you, right? I'm just nervous and that's why I snapped at you for calling Mildew."

"Pekie, I've had years of experience being your friend. I know you love me and I love you back."

Pekin smiled and stuffed her phone in the pocket of her

shorts. "I'll be back." Opening the door, she gasped when confronted with Mildew's upraised hand. "Oh! You scared me," she said.

"I was just about to knock. Hello, girls," the medium said. "Can I come in?"

Pekin nodded and stepped aside.

Mildew set down her handbag and looked around the room. "Where's Scout?"

"Scout's mad at Pekin," Amber offered. "He went for a walk."

"I'm not surprised," Mildew said. "I doubt he wants to take the chance of losing you again."

"He wouldn't lose me. Lily's not an evil spirit," Pekin said.

"Oh, sure," Amber said rolling her eyes. "She attacked you."

"She didn't *hurt* me," Pekin replied. "She was just mad."

"Geez, Pekin, what do you think an angry ghost is going to do, serve you milk and cookies?" Amber asked. "What do *you* think, Mildew?"

"Any time you're dealing with the spirit world, there are risks involved."

"What kind of risks?"

"Pekin already experienced one of the worst ones. George Trent is a perfect example."

"Lily wasn't a murderer," Pekin said.

"No, but what happens if she gets inside you and discovers she likes having a body again and doesn't want to leave?"

"She can do that?" Amber asked.

"She can. I'm not saying that's what will happen, but it's not out of the realm of possibility."

"How do we keep that from happening?" Pekin said.

"With a protection prayer," Mildew said. "I think allowing yourself to be inhabited by a spirit should be a last resort, after you've tried everything else."

Pekin's shoulders slumped. "This is impossible."

"Nothing's impossible," Mildew said with a reassuring smile. "Why don't you tell me about what's been going on here."

Amber launched into a spirited tale of the ghost looking for her baby, and detailed seeing the ghost on the second floor and various encounters with it, ending with Pekin's latest experience. "You want to go upstairs to see if you can tell if she's here?"

"Sure. I'll take a look around," Mildew said as she led the way upstairs.

At the top of the stairs, she closed her eyes and tried to feel whether any entities were present. After a moment, she said, "Nothing is here now."

When Scout returned fifteen minutes later, he was surprised to find Mildew sitting on the couch with Pekin and Amber.

"Did you talk her out of her ridiculous plan?" he asked pointedly.

"Not entirely, dear. I did make it clear that it should be a last resort, though."

That seemed to calm Scout down. He plopped into the recliner, making room for Spike to snuggle down beside him, and glared at Pekin, who sheepishly glanced away.

Amber looked back and forth between her friends. "This isn't helping," she said. "Pekin isn't going to go all *come on in, take over my brain* on us right away."

"Oh, funny, Amber," Scout said, with a scowl.

"Scout, dear," Mildew said. "In the event you all think it becomes necessary for Pekin to open herself to the energy in this house, I'll be here to make sure nothing bad happens."

"You can't promise nothing bad will happen, though, can you?" he asked.

Mildew held Scout's gaze. "No. I can't promise."

# Chapter Eighteen

A MBER'S PHONE PINGED. "It's a text from Mr. Grayson," she said.

"What does it say?" Pekin leaned closer to read the text.

"He's mad. Violet must have told him about us. He said he can't believe we approached his daughter and, if we don't stop, we'll be sorry."

"Text him back," Pekin said. "Here, let me." She took the phone out of Amber's hands.

*Why didn't you tell Violet about Lily?*

"You don't beat around the bush, do you?" Amber asked.

"We don't have time to beat around the bush. We've been here four days. We only have a few days left before the Dwyers come home. And, so far, we haven't made any progress at all."

"Let's see what he says," Mildew said.

Within moments, the phone dinged again.

*That's none of your business. Stay out of our lives.*

*We can't,* Pekin responded. *We can explain it all to you if you let us. I think you'll be interested in our reasons for contacting you.*

*There's nothing you can say to excuse your meddling.*

*There is, though.*

They waited a couple of minutes for a response, and Pekin typed out, *Mr. Grayson?*

Still no answer. In exasperation, Pekin typed, *We'll have to convince Violet, then.*

Instantly, the phone dinged. *If you persist in bothering my daughter, you'll regret it.*

*Then talk to us and let us explain. It has to do with Lily.*

*Lily's been gone for decades. I fail to see what she has to do with this.*

*I bet Violet would like to have the cradle Lily made for her.*

Pekin looked around at her friends. "If this doesn't get him to talk to us, I don't know what else we can do."

*How do you know about the cradle?*

*If you meet with us, we'll tell you everything. Please. It's important.*

They waited, watching the phone, which sat silent. Disappointed.

Ten minutes later, Mildew announced that it was time for her to leave and stood. She gave hugs all around and moved toward the front door.

At that moment, the phone pinged. Mildew waved once and continued out the door.

*Okay.*

"'Okay'. What does that mean?" an always excitable Amber asked.

Pekin waved her off. *When can you meet with us?* she typed.

A moment later the phone dinged, but it wasn't Ron Grayson.

"It's from the Dwyers," Pekin said. "They want to know how things are going here and if we've made any progress. What should I tell them?"

No one responded right away. "Wait. I know," Pekin said and started typing.

*We've found Lily's daughter, but haven't talked to her yet. Oh, Lily Grayson's your ghost. I think she may be skeptical. Her daughter, I mean. So I wondered if we could offer her Lily's cradle. We discovered that the baby cradle in your attic was hand painted by Lily for her daughter and thought her daughter might like to have it. If we can get her to come here, then Lily can see she's all right.*

"Um, did you really want to tell the Dwyers that we were poking around in their attic?" Scout asked grumpily.

Pekin glared at him. "*We* weren't poking around in their attic. It was Miranda."

"Does that change anything?" he responded.

Ding.

*You were in our attic?*

Scout looked at Pekin and raised his eyebrows.

Pekin shook her head and started typing. *We weren't. But Miranda...you remember Miranda, the ghost from our first case? She took a look up there to see if there might be clues. She found the cradle and told us about it. Then Claire told us about how Lily painted it for her daughter.*

*Really? Miranda was in our house?* Edie responded.

*Yes. She can be a big help at times.*

*Well, if you think Lily's daughter would want it, you can offer it to her.*

*Thank you so much. We're hoping to get this all wrapped up before you get back. Hope you're having fun.*

"Wow. That's so great," Amber said. "I was afraid they would be mad at us. It's lucky Edie finds Miranda so interesting. I'm sure Violet will want the cradle."

"Scout, I guess you'll have to go up and get it," Pekin said.

"Whatever," he groused. "We're almost out of cereal. I'm going to go get some more."

As he opened the front door, Pekin shot a worried glance at Amber and mouthed, *What should I do?*

*Go with him!* Amber mouthed back, giving Pekin a little shove.

"Wait for me," she called to Scout and hurried to catch the door before he pulled it shut behind him.

"Look, Pekin, I don't need your help to buy cereal."

"I know you don't, but..." She made her most pleading face. "Don't be mad at me, Scout. I don't really want to invite Lily to inhabit me, but I'm afraid we might have to."

He turned and looked at her, his eyes reflecting worry and anger and confusion. "What do you want from me?"

"I want you to take care of me if I have to do it. I *need* you, Scout."

"What do you think I can do about it if Lily won't leave?"

"You can be with me. I'll come back...for you." Pekin's cheeks turned red and she was unable to meet his eyes.

Scout took her hands. "You don't have to be embarrassed around me, Pekie."

She looked up at him. "I'm sorry I scared you."

"I just don't want to lose you. Last time was too awful."

"But it brought us together, didn't it?"

He pulled her into his arms and held her. "But what if it hadn't been enough?"

Pekin rested her head on his chest. "I know you'd never let anything happen to me," she whispered.

He stroked her hair. "Not if I can help it."

She looked up at him. "So, don't be mad at me, okay?"

He pulled back. "You can't expect me to be happy about you putting yourself in a dangerous situation."

"I won't, if I can help it." Her eyes pleaded with him. "I hope it doesn't come to that. So let's not worry about it unless we have to. Deal?"

He didn't answer immediately, clearly conflicted. "Fine. If we're going for cereal, let's go."

He didn't look at her as he opened his car door and slipped inside. Rolling down the window, he said, "You coming?"

"You can't be mad at me," Pekin said, climbing in the passenger side. "You're my boyfriend and you can't be mad at me."

"Guys get mad at their girlfriends all the time," he said, eyes on the road.

"Well, you're my first boyfriend and I don't like it." She crossed her arms and stared out the side window.

"So, you're never going to be mad at me?"

"I'm kind of mad at you right now. You're acting like a brat."

"This is really productive," he said. "Maybe you should just stay here."

She turned to face him. "I'm not staying here. I'm going with you." She turned toward the window again, then swung her head back around. "Always."

He started to retort, then smiled. "You're cute when you're mad."

"I am not," she huffed. But a small smile played at the corners of her mouth, and when he reached for her hand, she let him take it.

"So, are we okay?" she asked.

"We're good."

# Chapter Nineteen

"You guys, Mr. Grayson sent another text while you were gone," Amber said as soon as they walked in the front door.

"What did he say?" Pekin asked, taking the phone from Amber. Scout leaned in to read over her shoulder.

*I'm not happy that you've insinuated yourselves into our lives, but if meeting with you is what it will take for you to leave my daughter alone, then I'm willing to meet.*

"Wow," Scout said. "He's pretty unhappy with us."

"I feel bad," Amber said.

"Why?" Pekin asked. "We haven't done anything to him. You'd think he'd be happy we're trying to help his wife cross over."

"Sure, if he knew that's why we wanted to see him," Scout said.

"Well, it's not like we can just put it in a text," Pekin said, her warm feelings from the trip to the store with Scout flying right out the window.

She tapped her chin with her finger, thinking. *Hopefully you won't feel that way when you find out why we want to speak with you,* she typed.

*Then tell me why.*

*It's complicated. I promise we'll tell you everything when we see you. When can you meet with us? It would be really great if you could come here, to your old house on Firefly Lane. It will help you understand. If that's not possible, however, we're happy to meet with you wherever it's convenient for you.*

The three of them held their breath as they waited for a reply. At the phone's ding, all three let their breath out.

*If I can catch a flight this afternoon, maybe I can be there tonight. Does that work for you?*

*That would be great. We look forward to telling you everything.*

*And who's going to reimburse me for flying out there?*

Pekin looked at her friends in alarm. "What do I say?"

Then she bent her head over the phone and started typing. *We can discuss it when we see you. I don't think you'll be worrying about your travel expenses once you hear us out.*

*We'll see.*

Pekin looked up from the phone. "I guess we're on."

"I'm so nervous!" Amber said with a shiver.

"Me, too," Pekin admitted. She was silent for a minute, and said. "I'm going home for a while. My mom wants me to give her an update on what's happening, and, also, I want to pick up one of the newspaper articles about us so I can show Mr. Grayson in case he hasn't heard of us."

"Good idea, Pekie," Scout said.

"I guess I'll go home, too," Amber said. "What time should we be back?"

"Probably at least by 5:30. Maybe we can form a plan

for how we can get him on board," Pekin said. "Scout, can you take Spike out before you go? You know, since he likes you best. He's got to be antsy from being cooped up in the house all morning."

WHEN PEKIN'S MOM dropped her off shortly after five, Amber and Scout were already there. They convened in the family room to talk strategy. Unfortunately, coming up with a strategy for convincing someone a ghost wanted their daughter was a tall order. They settled on just telling the truth as they knew it and answering any questions he might have.

# Chapter Twenty

R ON GRAYSON ARRIVED about seven. His manner was gruff as the kids introduced themselves. Clearly, having had time to think about this meeting hadn't improved his view of it.

"Which one of you is Amber Crawford?" he asked with a scowl.

"Me," a clearly intimidated Amber responded.

"I'm Pekin Dewlap and this is Scout Levine."

Ron frowned. "So, what's this all about?"

When they were all seated in the family room, Pekin started. "Mr. Grayson, I know this is a very unusual situation." She ignored his glare. It unnerved her, and she seemed at a loss for words and glanced at Scout for help.

"In spite of the unconventional way we contacted you, there's a good reason for it," Scout said. "I wonder if you know who we are?"

"Other than a bunch of teenagers who are trying to blackmail me, no idea," Ron said, not lightening up.

"We aren't trying to blackmail you," Scout said. "But maybe, if you'll give us a chance to explain, you'll understand. The situation may be a little odd, but it's not a bad thing. We just need your help."

"There were some news reports about us a month or so ago," Pekin said. "We helped the police solve four cold cases."

Ron looked more interested. "Oh, yes. I remember reading about that."

Pekin handed him a copy of the news article and gave him a few minutes to scan it.

"What the news reports didn't really say was that the reason we were in that Elmwood house in the first place is because we were hired to get rid of a ghost that was haunting it."

Ron shook his head, his eyes rolling toward the ceiling. "Of all the—"

"Look. I know this is hard to accept, but there was a ghost in that house. In fact, there were two. We were able to get both of them removed. It was the ghost of the murderer who provided the information that led to the discovery of the remains of the four little girls. You may not believe us, but the police do. They were there when the murderer's ghost crossed over."

"You can't expect me to believe that."

"We're hoping you *will* believe it because that's indirectly why we needed to contact you." Scout pulled one of their business cards for The Ghost Company out of his wallet and handed it to Ron, who frowned and tossed it on the coffee table.

"Mr. Grayson," Pekin said, "your wife's ghost is haunting this house. She's looking for her baby."

"That's impossible," Ron said with a glare. "What the hell is really going on here?"

"Edie and Archie Dwyer, the couple who bought this house from you, called us because Lily is haunting this house. They're not scared of her, but Edie feels bad because Lily is so sad. She's always crying and asking for her baby. We thought...we were hoping...that, if Violet came here and showed Lily that she's all right, then Lily would be able to cross over."

"I am not exposing my daughter to this craziness," Ron said, standing up.

Scout put up a hand. "Please, Mr. Grayson, just hear us out. We've seen Lily ourselves. She's angry and sad, and we really want to help her move on. Maybe if you could see her yourself you'd understand."

Ron huffed. "Okay. I give up. Where is she?"

"Well, she's usually upstairs, but we can't be sure she'll come out now."

"That's what I thought," Ron said. "Are you running some kind of scam?"

"Why doesn't Violet know about Lily?" Amber interjected. "She doesn't know her own mother?"

Ron spun on Amber. "That's none of your business, and I want you to stay out of my daughter's life."

"We can't help Lily without your daughter's help," Pekin said. "If you'll just give us a chance, we can prove to you that Lily's really here."

Scout shot Pekin a look. "Pekin, no."

"It might be the only way, Scout," she pleaded.

Spike, who was curled up at Scout's feet, suddenly lifted his head and growled softly. When he jumped to his feet and ran barking to the foot of the stairs, all eyes followed him.

"He only acts like that when Lily's here," Amber said.

"Maybe she feels your presence," Pekin said to Ron.

He started to protest when the eerie, hollow sound of sobbing floated down the stairs. "What's that?" he asked.

"It's Lily."

He turned his glare on Pekin. "I don't know what scam you're trying to pull on me, but I have a mind to report you to the police."

"Please do," Scout said. "In fact, you can contact Captain Burroughs or Officer Elliott of the Springdale Police Department. They were the officers who investigated the cold cases and located the remains of the girls. They'll vouch for us."

*Where's my baby* sounded from the second floor. Ron's face whipped toward the stairs.

"Lily?" he said softly.

"Come on, let's go," Scout said already heading for the stairway.

All of them scrambled up the stairs, with Spike waiting at the bottom, barking.

"Do you feel the chill? That's the sign a spirit is present," Scout said over his shoulder. A shimmer appeared at the far end of the hallway and glided toward them. "There," Scout pointed.

Ron watched the shimmer as it moved past them and disappeared into one of the bedrooms.

*I want my baby* echoed from the room and the sobs grew louder.

Ron ran into the bedroom. "Where is she?"

When the kids followed him into the room, Pekin said, "She's gone. It's already getting warm in here."

"That's convenient," Ron said. "How did you do that?"

Scout sighed in exasperation. "We didn't do anything. We're telling you that Lily's spirit is trapped here and she can't move on until she's reconnected with Violet."

"You kids are ridiculous," Ron snarled, turning and taking the stairs two at a time. "Don't bother me or my daughter again or you'll hear from my lawyer."

"What's wrong with you?" Amber asked. "What kind of man listens to his wife's despair and turns his back on her?" She glared at him. "You're an awful man."

"Amber, let him go," Pekin said. "We knew he'd have a hard time believing us."

"I don't care. He saw her. He heard her. He even said her name like he recognized her. Now, he's accusing us of staging a fake magic trick? I feel sorry for Lily that she had such a cold, unfeeling husband." Amber stomped out of the room.

Ron watched her go, his mouth hanging open, the air out of his sails. "I loved my wife. I moved out of this house because I couldn't bear being here without her."

"Why didn't you tell Violet about her mother then?" Pekin asked.

Ron's shoulders slumped and he sank into a chair in the family room. "A year after Lily's death, I met a wonderful woman who doted on Violet. When we were married, we decided it would be confusing to a baby to keep hearing about a dead woman that the baby would never know. She convinced me to let her adopt Violet. Andrea was a good woman, a good mother, and we never told Violet that Andrea wasn't her biological mother." He looked at his folded hands. "Maybe it was wrong, but Violet was happy, and she loved Andrea. After a while, it seemed pointless to confuse a child with tales of a mother she didn't know."

"What about Lily's family?" Pekin asked. "Don't they have a right to know she had a baby? Her parents would have loved to know there was a grandchild for them to love. It was very unfair of you—"

Ron rubbed a hand over his face. "Lily had no family. Except me. Her parents were killed in a car accident before we were married. She didn't have any siblings."

"Oh." Pekin paused, thinking. "What about her birth certificate?"

"We showed it to her when she was still a little girl. By the time she was grown up, she'd forgotten about it. When she applied for a passport, I had her fill out the paperwork but went with her to the passport office and handed the clerk the birth certificate myself, then took it back and put it in my pocket."

"Didn't she want a copy for herself?" Scout asked.

"She mentioned it, and I told her I'd get her a copy, but never quite got around to it. If she'd ever made an issue out of it, I'd have been forced to tell her about Lily."

"Don't you think it's time she knew?" Pekin asked.

Amber, who'd returned to the family room, still glared at Ron. "Yeah, I'd be really mad if I found out my whole life was a lie."

"Her life wasn't a lie," Ron said, looking at Amber. "Andrea was a wonderful mother who couldn't have loved Violet more if she were her biological daughter. It wouldn't have changed anything if she knew. She'd still have had Andrea for a mother." His shoulders slumped. "And...something else. Lily died in my arms. I've always blamed myself, that maybe there was something I could have done to save her. I guess the guilt...I don't know. Maybe I was worried Violet would blame me."

"I don't think she would have," Pekin said. "How could you have saved Lily? You aren't a doctor."

Ron silently shook his head, a defeated look in his eyes.

"Where's Andrea?" Scout asked. "Maybe the two of you could talk to Violet together."

"Andrea died of cancer three years ago," Ron said, a tear sliding down his cheek. "I don't want Violet to hate Andrea, especially when Andrea isn't here to defend herself."

"So, what? You're just going to let Lily continue to wander the halls of this house crying for her baby?" Amber asked, her arms firmly crossed over her chest. "Because you don't want to be honest with your daughter?"

"What good would it do anybody?" Ron pleaded.

"How can you even ask that?" Amber shouted.

Pekin and Scout looked at her, confused. "What's going on, Amber?" Pekin asked. "Why are you so upset about this?"

Amber turned her back, crossing her arms in anger. "I don't want to talk about it."

"Come on, Amber. Something's wrong," Pekin said. "Spill."

Amber turned back, her eyes red. "Because," she said, bursting into tears. "Because my Aunt Sharon died when my cousin Nancy was a baby. Even though Nancy didn't really remember my aunt, she always, always loved her. Nancy stayed with us a lot when we were growing up, for my mom's sake as well as her own. Nancy was one of my best friends, and still is. Let me tell you, if Nancy's mother was unable to go to heaven and she could help her and didn't, she wouldn't have been able to live with herself. Even though Nancy has a wonderful stepmother, who's been in her life since she was two, Nancy still loves her mother. She'd feel cheated if she'd been lied to. It would be like her real mom never existed. And that's what you're doing to Violet," she finished, jabbing her finger at Ron.

"I didn't know that," Scout said, scooting next to Amber and putting an arm around her.

"You told me a long time ago, but I forgot," Pekin said. "I'm sorry for being a bad friend."

"You're not a bad friend. Nancy has had a happy, secure life, and loves her stepmom. You're my best friend and I love you," she said, squeezing Pekin's hand and wiping her eyes. She turned to Ron. "I'm sorry. I shouldn't have put that on you."

Ron hung his head. "What do I do now?"

Scout sighed. "You know what we think you should do. You need to tell Violet and see if you can get her to come here to set her mother free."

Ron looked miserable. "I don't know how to do that. I don't want her to hate me, either."

"You had your reasons for keeping her in the dark. Maybe she'll understand," Pekin said.

"I need to think about it," Ron said.

Amber shook her head. "What's to think about? Lily needs you to do this!"

"I have to go," Ron said, standing.

The kids watched him leave, not knowing what would happen next. They flopped down on the couch, heavy sighs from all of them.

"I think he'll do the right thing," Pekin said, but no one piped in to agree with her.

"Let's get some dinner," Scout said. "We've done all we can for now."

# Chapter Twenty-One

~~~~~~~~~~~~~~~~~~~~~~~~~~~~~~~~~~~~~~~~~~~~~~~~~

THEY WERE ALL STILL SLEEPING around the family room. No one felt like talking much after dinner, until Pekin announced that she needed to practice her meditating.

Scout's face grew bright red. Before he could say anything, Pekin said, "Don't freak out on me, Scout. We have to be prepared for whatever we need to do."

"I still don't think you need to do that!"

"It's just one option. Maybe it won't come to that. But, if it does, I want to be ready."

"She might be right," Amber said. "Lily isn't interacting with us the way Miranda did."

"I can't believe you guys are willing to take chances like this," Scout said. "Go ahead and go meditate. I'm going to take a shower."

Pekin and Amber looked at each other as Scout headed for the bathroom. Pekin's face reflected her concern that he was so upset with her. "It's not like I really want to do it," she pleaded to Amber.

"I know, and I really hope you don't have to."

"Well, you know, all our eggs are in the Ron basket," Pekin said. "We don't really have another plan. What if he doesn't come through for us?"

"Yeah. Now that you mention it, we are kind of betting on Ron. But I'm sure he's going to do the right thing," Amber said. "I mean, I might have shamed him into it."

Pekin gave a weak laugh. "You kinda did." She stood up. "I'm going to go out on the back patio and spend some time trying to meditate. Tell Scout I'm sorry, when he comes back."

Amber shot her a worried look. "I will, but he's pretty upset. He may not want to hear it."

"You can send him out, then. I'll try to make him understand."

Amber looked skeptical, but said, "Okay."

Once Pekin had positioned herself in a prone position on one of the patio chaises, she had a difficult time clearing her mind of her worry over Scout. She sighed and did her best to think of nothing, but grew more dejected as each moment passed without a feeling of peace. "I need Mildew," she said.

"At the least," Scout said from the backdoor.

"Oh, Scout," Pekin said, sitting up. "Please don't be mad at me. I can't stand it when you're mad."

"What do you want me to feel, Pekie? You're putting yourself in danger and all I can do is stand back and watch. Don't you care about me at all?"

"You know I do. I lo—"

Suddenly shy, Pekin didn't finish. She couldn't say the "L" word. What if it ruined everything? And he hadn't said it to her. But she did have deep feelings for Scout, and she hoped he knew that.

She cleared her throat. "What choice do I have? If Lily can't hear our words, or refuses to hear our words, how will we help her cross over? What if Violet comes here and stands in the baby's room and says 'I'm here' and Lily doesn't believe her. Don't you see? Letting her communicate through me might be the only way to connect her to her family."

A tear slid down her cheek, and she brushed it away. "I'm sorry, Scout. Please don't worry about me. Mildew won't let anything bad happen."

The anxiety on her face caused Scout to sit next to her on the chaise and put his arms around her. He buried his face in the crook of her neck.

"Oh, Scout," she said. She lifted his face and looked into his eyes. And kissed him.

He sighed as he kissed her back, then pulled back and looked at her with wonder in his eyes. Then he kissed her again.

When she finally pulled away, she said, "Our first kiss." Blushing, she added, "It was wonderful."

He laughed. "For me, too. Thanks, Pekie. I needed that."

Everything felt different to Pekin. Like her relationship with Scout was real.

He stood and smiled crookedly. "Look, don't worry about me. If you feel like you need to channel Lily, I'll be there to save you if anything goes wrong."

"Thanks, Scout," Pekin said, her heart on her sleeve. "I'm so happy."

He laughed and headed back inside.

Now it was even more difficult for Pekin to clear her mind of thoughts. How could she erase the memory of kissing Scout?

OVER CORNFLAKES the next morning, the kids mostly ate in silence, Pekin and Scout not looking up from their cereal.

"How did your meditating go?" Amber asked Pekin.

Pekin blushed. "Not very well. I couldn't concentrate."

"Why not? And why are you blushing?"

Pekin squirmed and Amber gave her the side eye.

"What's wrong?" Amber asked.

"Nothing's wrong. I just couldn't do it."

"Why not?"

"*I* don't know. I just couldn't."

Amber contemplated her friend. "Something's changed." She wiggled her eyebrows. "Come on. What happened? Tell Auntie Amber everything."

Pekin turned bright red from her head to her toes. Scout frowned at Amber. "What are you going on about? Nothing's changed."

"Yeah, sure." Amber wiggled her eyebrows again. "Did you two *make up?*" she asked, making air quotes.

"Scout's not mad at me anymore," Pekin said, not meeting Amber's eyes.

"Yeah. So drop it," Scout added.

"Okay, if that's how you want it. But, just so you know, *I* know."

"I don't know what you think you know," Scout said, carrying his bowl over to the sink to rinse out.

"Oh, nothing," Amber teased. "So, what do we do now?" she asked while carrying her bowl to the sink, too. "Or do you two want to be alone?" Amber's smile was wicked.

Pekin threw up her hands. "I give up."

"You do?" Amber asked.

"Scout and I kissed. That's all."

Amber pumped her fist. "I *knew* it! Now we can double date after all and it won't be awkward."

"Whatever," Scout said, stomping out of the kitchen.

He was back a minute later, his backpack slung over his shoulder. "I'm going home for a while. My mom has some chores she wants me to do. I'll be back this afternoon." He looked at Amber, then at Pekin, and stepped closer and kissed Pekin before he turned and left.

Pekin blushed and Amber grinned. A huge grin.

"So...That happened."

"Yes. Now we're officially boyfriend and girlfriend. Can you just drop it?"

"Come on, bestie. You know you want to tell me everything. How did it make you feel? I'm dying to know. Tell me! Tell me!"

Pekin really *did* want to tell her best friend everything. So she sighed and said, "It was amazing."

"How did it happen? Did he pull you into his arms and kiss you?"

"No. I kissed him."

"Way to go, Pekie!"

"He said he was sorry and that if I wanted to channel Lily he'd be there in case anything went wrong. But, Amber, he looked so sad. It broke my heart. I just *had* to kiss him. And he kissed me back."

"Yes!" Amber pulled Pekin into a big hug.

"And that's all there is to it. We're still going to take it slow."

"Yeah, sure. But I don't know how much slower you can take it."

Pekin glared. "Look. This is all new still. I mean, only a month ago I thought Scout was into Vanessa Dooley."

"I remember. You were psychotic about Vanessa."

"I was not. I just...I was jealous, that's all."

"But now you know he's into you."

"I know. But I'm scared. What if, after we start dating, he decides I'm not what he wants?"

"Scout has known you for *years*. He knows who you are, and he knows you're who he wants. So, that's the last thing you should worry about."

"I can't help it. I mean, I've never had a boyfriend before."

"Neither have I, but Josh and I figured it out pretty quickly. And having a boyfriend is great."

"Okay. But don't push me." Pekin blushed and smiled a small smile. "I'm really happy, though."

"I'm so happy *for* you."

"Please don't tease Scout."

"What fun is that? It's so easy!"

"Yeah, well, if you want me to keep you in the loop, you better be cool about this."

Amber shook her head. "Okay. Fine." But she threw her arms around Pekin. "I love you."

"I love you, too."

Pekin's eyes dropped.

"Uh oh," Amber said. "What is it?"

"It's nothing. Okay, it isn't nothing...I almost told Scout I loved him."

"Why didn't you?"

"Because. Because what if he doesn't feel the same way?"

"What are you talking about? He saved your life. He got all beat up by that ghost, and he did it to protect you. What about that makes you think he's not into you?"

"But we just started to be together. Isn't it too soon?"

"Only if you make it weird. You just told me you love me. You've told Scout you love him a million times, so what's the problem now?"

"Well, I never told him I *love* love him. It's too scary."

"I have faith in you, girlfriend. You'll know when the time is right."

"Have you told Josh you love him?" Pekin asked.

"No." Amber looked thoughtful. "But I haven't known Josh inside and out like you know Scout. I haven't spent years as his best friend. We have to work up to the 'L' word."

"That makes sense. I just hope Scout and I can be as comfortable around each other as you and Josh are."

"Now that you got the first kiss out of the way, it'll be easy. Just be yourself, Pekie. That's the person he loves."

Pekin rinsed out her breakfast bowl. "Let's go upstairs and see if Lily's around."

"Spike's not barking and it's not cold in here, so I doubt it. I guess it doesn't hurt to check, though."

Of course, there was no Lily in the upstairs hallway. Pekin called her name a few times and said they needed to talk to her, but didn't get a response, so she and Amber went back down to the family room.

"What do we do now?" Pekin asked.

Amber slumped back on the couch, her arms crossed over her chest, looking thoughtful. "I guess I should go see if my mom needs anything."

"Maybe I should, too. Besides, Griselda probably misses me."

"She's a cat. She's probably sleeping through your absence."

"Probably. Still, I miss her. Spike's no replacement for my sweet little Griselda."

"Speaking of Spike, should we take him out before we go?" Amber asked.

"Sure. A short walk will be good for all of us."

# Chapter Twenty-Two

P EKIN WAS LYING ON HER BED reading with Griselda curled up on her stomach when her phone pinged with a message from Amber.

*Ron texted to say he talked to Violet today and offered to bring her by tonight. Cool, huh?*

*Yes. Text Scout and tell him. I'll get my mom to give me a ride back to the house.*

Pekin texted Mildew that tonight was the night for contacting Lily and asked if she could be there. Just in case.

After getting a yes from Mildew, Pekin stuffed her Kindle in her backpack and asked her mom for a ride to Firefly Lane.

Pekin was the first one back. Scout's car wasn't parked out front, and, when Pekin opened the front door and called out, no one but Spike answered. She let him out of the kitchen, where he was usually corralled when no one was home, and attached his leash so she could take him out for a quick walk before her friends got back.

SCOUT AND AMBER ARRIVED as she was unlocking the front door, and Spike was beside himself with joy when he spotted Scout.

Scout stooped down and Spike jumped into his arms for a ride into the house. Pekin and Amber watched them go. "He's so adorable," Amber said.

"You mean Spike, right?" Pekin said.

"You know what I mean," Amber said, and winked.

"Yes. He is."

Once they were inside and gathered in the family room, Pekin asked Scout if he would get the cradle down from the attic. She followed him upstairs as he examined the panel in the second floor ceiling. It wasn't painted shut, but obviously hadn't been opened in a very long time. There was a small hole in one end, which was probably where a tool was used to lower the stairs.

He looked at Pekin. "So, where would you be if you were an attic tool?"

She laughed. "Probably in a closet in one of the spare bedrooms. You take one room and I'll take the other."

The closets in both rooms were obviously used for storage and Pekin faced a wall of clutter when she opened hers. "Is yours as stuffed as mine is?" she called out to Scout.

"Yeah. I wouldn't have thought the Dwyers were packrats."

"Probably a lot of the stuff belongs to their kids," she said.

As she carefully pushed aside items searching for a pole, she could hear Scout shuffling through his closet.

"I found it!" he called.

They met in the hallway under the attic, Scout proudly waving a wooden pole with a metal hook on one end.

Pekin held her breath as he inserted the hook in the attic door and pulled it down, the stairs unfolding in front of them.

"I want to see, too," she said as Scout climbed up into the attic.

"It's pretty dusty. And super-hot. But come on up."

Scout was wiping his forehead with the bottom of his T-shirt when she joined him in the attic. It didn't take more than a minute before she was fanning her face. "It's like a furnace up here."

"Let's make this fast," he said. He shined around the flashlight he'd stuck in his back pocket.

"There," he said, focusing the light on the cradle. The attic was fairly empty. It didn't look like the Dwyers had found a need to stash a bunch of junk up there. Along the wall behind the cradle were several cardboard boxes.

Pekin examined the boxes, not wanting to touch anything because of the thick dust, but after a moment, she said, "One of the boxes has some writing on it. Can you shine the light over here?"

The word *Lily* was written on it in black Sharpie. "Bring that down, too, okay?" she said.

"I'm gonna need you to go back down so I can hand the cradle to you. I don't think I can manage it and the stairs, too," Scout said.

Pekin took another look around the attic and climbed down the stairs. "I'm ready," she said.

She heard scuffling from the attic. "It's not too heavy," Scout's voice drifted down to her. "But it's super awkward. I'll hold onto my end and you can ease it down."

"Okay," she said, while over her shoulder she called out to Amber. "Can you come help us?"

Amber was at Pekin's side in a moment. One end of the cradle was already coming through the attic opening and Pekin and Amber reached up to guide it down.

"Eww. It's really grungy," Amber said, wrinkling her nose and sneezing.

"We have to clean it up before Ron and Violet get here," Pekin said.

"You ready?" Scout called down, sliding the cardboard box toward the opening.

"Yep," Pekin said.

The box was surprisingly light, covered with a layer of dust. "Can you carry the cradle out to the backyard?" Pekin asked as he hopped off the last step. "I'll get the box. We need to clean them off out there so we don't make a mess in the house."

"No problem." Scout hefted the cradle and crab-walked with it down the stairs and out the backdoor.

Amber joined them out back armed with window cleaner and paper towels. She and Pekin got to work de-griming the cradle.

"It's pretty, isn't it?" Pekin said. "I bet Violet will love it."

"Depends on how Ron's story went over with her. She could be angrier than he was when he was here," Scout said.

"I can't think about that now. We have to make tonight work. The Dwyers will be back on Saturday, and we need to be able to show them we were successful."

"*If* we're successful," Amber said. "I just don't see how we'll convince Ron and Violet."

"Don't sell us short, Amber," Pekin said, giggling. "We've got *skills*."

"*I'm* not feeling so skillful. Lily won't even talk to us."

"That's why Mildew's coming over," Pekin said, before sparing a sheepish glance toward Scout.

He smartly didn't respond.

"She's coming over around five," Pekin said, brushing dust out of her hair. "I'm hoping she has some advice for us."

"Like what?" Amber asked.

"I don't know, but if Lily doesn't come out, Mildew might be able to help us contact her."

"Her take might be different from ours," Scout said. "She's been doing this kind of thing for a long time."

"How does this look?" Pekin asked, standing back and indicating the cradle.

"It's uhh-dorable," Amber said, drawing out the word. "How could she not want it?"

Pekin turned her attention to the cardboard box. She dampened another couple of paper towels with window cleaner and rubbed most of the grime off the top, then drug the box over to the rustic patio table so she could sit while going through it.

There were several pictures of Lily, Lily and Ron, and a few other unidentified people. A wedding photo album. Pekin flipped the pages. "How cool to see what Lily looked like when she was alive. She was really pretty, and she looked so happy on her wedding day," she said. "We have to give these to Violet."

Pekin passed the album and photos around, and dove back into the box.

She looked up, disappointed. "There's not much here. Just some folded up clothes and a baby book."

"That might be something," Amber said, sitting beside Pekin on the redwood bench.

Pekin examined the padded satin cover of the book. Pink and blue unicorns danced on the ivory-colored front, around the title "Baby's First Year". She opened the book, not expecting to find any entries, but on the first page Lily had written a note to her future baby:

*I'm going to call you Violet. Your father keeps saying we don't know if you'll be a girl or a boy, but I feel in my heart that you'll be the sweetest little girl. The days seem so long until I can meet you. I already love you with all my heart. I have so many hopes for you. I know you'll be beautiful and generous and good. Because I know your soul. I will fill this book with pictures of you, and there's a special page for your little footprints and hand prints. I wonder how much you'll weigh. I know you'll fill my arms just right. No little baby in the whole world will be loved more than you will be, my darling. I'll keep all my memories of you in this book, and when you're all grown up and starting your own life, I'll give it to you, and you'll know how loved you are.*

Pekin's eyes welled up. "Poor Lily. It's so unfair that she never got to hold her baby."

Amber was blubbering. She sniffled and dug a tissue out of a pocket.

"You guys are so emotional," Scout said with a grin, turning away to wipe his own eyes.

"Well, you're just unsentimental," Amber said. "Anybody with a heart would shed a tear after reading that."

Pekin flipped through the rest of the small book. There was one more entry. She started reading aloud.

*Only a few more days, my love. My heart is bursting at the thought of seeing you. I can hardly wait. Your father has been wonderful. You're so lucky to have him for a dad. I love him so much, and I know you will, too.*

"The handwriting got jagged here," Pekin said, looking up, and continued.

*I want you to have…*

"She stopped there," Pekin said. "In the middle of a sentence. Do you think that's when she suddenly went into labor?"

"It's possible. She said she was within days of her due date," Amber said. "Is there a date on the entry?"

"Yes. The first one was dated May 25 and this one was June 2. If we knew what Violet's birthday is, we'd know for sure. Maybe she'll tell us."

"It's even sadder now," Amber said, wiping her eyes with the tissue.

"Yes, but it shows how much Lily loved her daughter. I'm sure Violet will be comforted by that."

"If she's not too mad to read it," Scout said. "I can't imagine that Ron's conversation with her went well."

"Maybe he's a good explainer," Amber said.

"I guess we'll find out soon," Scout said.

Amber knelt by the cradle. "I wish we had some ribbon. It would be so cool if we could put a big bow on the cradle." She glanced at Pekin, then turned to Scout and said, "Can you drive me to the drugstore to get some?"

"Sure. If it will make you crybabies happy," he said with a wink.

"You're *so* caring," Amber said, sticking out her tongue at him.

"You need anything while we're out?" he asked Pekin.

"I don't think so. But hurry back. I'm really nervous and I don't want to be here alone if they arrive early."

Scout laughed and gave her a bear hug. "I'll hurry." He kissed the top of her head.

Pekin watched after him as he closed the front door behind him, a dreamy look on her face. *I'm so lucky*, she thought.

She glanced at the time on her phone. It was already 4:30. It wouldn't be long before she'd be on deck. She shivered at the thought of Lily's spirit inhabiting her, then squared her shoulders and headed into the kitchen for a bottle of water. Whatever was going to happen, she was just along for the ride.

# Chapter Twenty-Three

~~~~~~~~~~~~~~~~~~~~~~~~~~~~~~~~~~~~~~~~~~~~~~~~

"**Y**OO HOO**,**" Pekin heard at the same time there was a knock at the front door. When she opened it, Mildew apologized for being early.

Pekin was glad to see her, though, and led Mildew to a seat in the family room. "Can I get you something to drink? We have bottled water and soda. I can even make tea if you want some."

"I'm fine, dear," Mildew said. "I brought my tools of the trade with me," she continued, indicating the tote bag she'd dropped at her feet. "I have my EMP reader, salt, sage. Whatever we might need." She noticed the anxiety in Pekin's eyes. "Everything is going to be fine. Is Scout still unhappy about you and Lily merging?"

"Actually, he said he's okay with whatever I think I need to do. He even said he'd save me again if he needed to."

Mildew patted her hand. "I'm glad. It will make things much less tense if you're not worrying about upsetting your young man."

"Thanks, Mildew. I feel better already just having you here."

"Have you seen much of Lily's spirit?"

"Not really." Pekin shivered. "I've called for her, but she either didn't hear me or didn't want to show herself. What if she doesn't come out while the Graysons are here?"

"Then we'll have to clear our minds and try to will her into appearing."

"Will that work?"

"I certainly hope so. It often does." Mildew searched through her tote bag and brought out a white candle. "Now, don't fret about it. We'll cross that bridge when we come to it."

"What's the candle for?" Pekin asked.

"That's to concentrate your mind if we need to go that route."

The front door burst open and Amber rushed in to give Mildew a big hug. "Did Pekin show you the cradle? It's so cool. We cleaned it up so it sparkles."

Mildew smiled. "Not yet, but I can't wait to see it."

"We bought ribbons so we can make it look like a present," Amber said.

"Hi, Mildew," Scout said. "I'm glad you're here."

"I am, too. You can't be too careful."

"That's what I keep telling Pekin, but she's kinda hard-headed." He grinned at Pekin.

She laughed. "I guess I am, kinda."

"We have to get everything wrapped," Amber said, waving the plastic drugstore bag. "Come on, Pekie."

Mildew trailed after them as they moved through the house and out the backdoor. The cradle was sitting on the porch. Mildew agreed that it was lovely, and watched as Amber and Pekin wrapped up the wedding album and the baby book, with the photos tucked inside, and set the package inside the cradle. Then, they attached a big red bow with streamers to the top of the cradle. Pekin helped Scout carry it up to the guest bedroom next to the master, which everyone agreed would have probably been the nursery.

"That looks so great!" Amber said. "I'm getting excited."

"I'm getting nervous," Pekin said, putting a hand on her stomach. "I think my tummy's upset."

"I'll get you a soda," Scout said, heading for the kitchen. When he came back with a Sprite, he said, "This should make you feel better. Can't help with your nerves, though."

Pekin gratefully took a couple of sips of the Sprite. "Thanks. I feel better already."

"Do you all want to discuss anything before the Graysons arrive?" Mildew asked. "You probably have questions."

They all filed back into the family room. "Yeah. Tell us how to do it," Pekin said.

"Without the need for an exorcist, if possible," Scout said.

"I have a feeling everything's going to be okay," Mildew said, patting his hand.

"So, what do we do if she doesn't come out?" Amber asked, scrutinizing a chip in her pink manicured nails.

"We can try to contact her. We need to go to the room where she most likely visits and then quietly ask her to come."

"Should we use a Ouija board?" Amber asked.

"No. I definitely don't recommend using a Ouija board. They can be dangerous. Things besides the ghost you're trying to contact can come through. Then you have more entities to get rid of."

"We don't want that," Pekin said, shivering at the thought of more entities like George making it through.

There was a shimmer in the room and Miranda appeared. *I came in case you need me,* she said.

"That might be helpful," Mildew said. "Nice to see you, Miranda."

"Yeah, thanks," Pekin said.

The sound of a car door caught their attention and Amber pushed aside the curtain in the front window and looked out. "It's Ron and Violet."

"I guess we're up," Pekin said, taking a deep breath. She opened the door as they were walking up to the porch.

"Hi," she said, stepping aside and waving them inside.

A nervous Ron cleared his throat and introduced his daughter.

Each of Pekin's team reintroduced themselves.

Violet looked around, her expression blank. "I still don't know why you came to my house," she said to Pekin.

"Well, we thought—"

"And I don't know why I'm here. I find out that my mom isn't really my mom and that my *real* mom died in childbirth. Now, I'm in some stranger's house." Violet glared at her father. "Why am I at this house? I don't remember it at all and don't know why you'd think I had any interest in seeing it now."

"Didn't you tell her about——" Amber started.

"Uh, no. I didn't really know how."

Pekin sighed in frustration. "So, you're leaving that part up to us?"

"Why don't we all sit down," Mildew said. "We have a lot to talk about."

# Chapter Twenty-Four

"**C**AN I GET YOU ANYTHING?" Pekin asked, attempting to be a good host. "Water, soda? I can put water on for tea or make some coffee."

"I could use something stronger," Ron said, rubbing a hand over his face.

"I don't know whether—"

"I was just kidding," Ron said. "I don't think we need anything. Let's just get this over with."

Pekin took a deep breath. "So, you were born in this house. And your mother died in this house."

"I know all that. My dad told me everything. It still doesn't explain why I had to come here."

"Your dad didn't tell you everything. Your mother is still here."

"What are you talking about?" Violet snapped.

Pekin glanced at Scout for help. He cleared his throat. "We told your dad all this, but now we're telling you. Your mother's spirit is still in this house. The Dwyers, who own the house now, called us to help her cross over." He pulled out one of their business cards and handed it to her.

"The Ghost Company? Are you kidding me?"

"No, actually, I'm not kidding. I don't know if you heard about the case last month where the bodies of four children were located after being missing for a century?"

Violet narrowed her eyes. "Yeah. So?"

"So, we're the ones who told the police where to find the bodies. And the reason we knew where to find them is because the ghost of the murderer took over Pekin's body and showed her what he'd done."

Violet closed her eyes and shook her head. "Okay. I give up. What is it you want from me that I just *had* to be in this house?" She glared at Scout. "Not that I'm buying one word of it."

"That's up to you, of course," Scout said. "Your mother's spirit is haunting this house because she's looking for you."

Violet crossed her arms over her chest, her mouth a tight line.

"Oh, my God," Amber piped in. "Stop being so… so…mean. We're trying to help your mother move on. She thinks her baby's lost because she died in childbirth and never got to hold you. So now she wanders the halls searching for you, crying because she can't find you. All you have to do is let her know you're here and that you're okay. I'd think you'd want to help your own mother."

"I told you about that one," Ron said to his daughter.

"Yeah, you did." Violet turned her glare back to Amber. "First of all, today is the first day I've even heard of my *real* mother. I didn't even know Andrea wasn't my birth mom. So don't put it on me."

"If you only knew how much Lily loved you," Amber said, glaring right back. "maybe you'd be a little more sympathetic. You meant everything to her."

"And you know that how?" Violet asked, not softening her stance at all.

"You're kind of a witch, you know that?" Amber said, clearly angry.

"Amber," Mildew said, putting a hand on her arm, "Violet hasn't had a chance to process the new information her father gave her. You need to give her a break."

Amber looked at Violet, thunderclouds in her eyes, but sank back in the couch, her arms tightly crossed over her chest.

"Violet," Pekin said, "the reason we know your mother loved you is because we found the baby book she kept where she wrote notes to you. We have that for you. We also have the cradle she spent days painting to get ready for you. Do you want to see them?"

Violet looked skeptical but nodded.

"They're up in the room that we think used to be your nursery," Pekin said. "Shall we go up?"

"Okay," Violet said, looking like she'd rather be anywhere else.

Everyone stood and followed Pekin upstairs and into the guest bedroom located next to the master. Pekin put a tentative hand on Violet's arm. "Here you are."

Violet stared at the beautiful cradle the kids had worked so hard on to clean away years of grime. She stood silently, not moving, as Ron approached the cradle and reached out his hand to touch it. "I remember this. I'd forgotten how lovely it was. She put so much work into it." His voice broke.

Violet watched for a moment, then hugged him. She noticed the giftwrapped package resting in the bed of the cradle and picked it up.

"Is this——"

"Yes," Pekin said. "That's the baby book your mom kept. She meant to fill in every page, but didn't get the chance. There are some pictures of her, as well." She glanced at Ron. "Your wedding album is also there."

Ron rubbed his nose, stifling a sniffle.

Violet sank down on the bed and stared at the package in her lap. After a moment, she removed the giftwrap and ran her hand over the cover of the baby book. She set the wedding album aside and, with a sigh, opened the baby book and picked up the photos. She took a couple of moments to study them. "So that's her?"

She handed the pictures to her father. Ron ran a finger over a picture of Lily smiling into the camera. "She was beautiful, wasn't she?"

"She was," Violet said absently as she read the first entry in the book.

With wonder in her voice, Violet said, "I know how she felt because I have a daughter, too. I could have written these words to her." She flipped to the next, shorter, entry. When she looked up, her eyes were wide. "June 2nd is my birthday."

Ron sat beside her on the bed. "I'm glad you got to see

this. I could tell you a hundred times that Lily loved you, but it wouldn't have the same impact as seeing it firsthand in your mother's handwriting."

"Dad, she stopped in the middle of a sentence. She was writing to me when she went into labor," Violet said. "And then she died."

She knelt by the cradle and touched it gently. "Can I have it?" she asked.

"Yes," Pekin said. "We already asked the Dwyers and they said it's rightfully yours."

"I appreciate it." Violet's eyes hardened. "But I still don't believe that she's haunting this house. Ghosts aren't real."

"But they are," Amber said. "We've seen them. We've talked to them."

"You're delusional, then," she said.

"And you're still a witch," Amber replied.

"Amber!" Pekin said. "That isn't helping."

"She doesn't believe us," Amber said.

"Of course I don't believe you," Violet said. "If she's here, where is she?"

"She's not here right now," Pekin said. "She isn't always around."

"Kind of convenient, wouldn't you say?"

"Violet," Ron said. "I'm not sure they're wrong. When I was here before, I thought I heard Lily's voice."

"*Thought* is the operative word here, Dad," she said. "Ghosts aren't real."

Pekin shrugged. "Miranda, can you come help us out?"

"Who's Miranda?" Violet asked.

# Chapter Twenty-Five

~~~~~~~~~~~~~~~~~~~~~~~~~~~~~~~~~~~~~~~~~~~~~~~~~~~~~~~~~~~~~

"SHE IS," AMBER SAID, pointing to the shimmer that slowly took shape as a young girl.

"Oh, my God," Violet said. Her hand flying to her mouth, she shrank against her dad.

*Hello*, Miranda said.

Eyes wide, Violet looked at her, and buried her face in Ron's shoulder. "Get it away from me!"

"How rude" Amber said. "Miranda's not an *it*. "She's a girl...ghost."

"It's okay," Pekin said. "Miranda is our friend. She won't hurt you."

"Yeah," Amber added. "Since you didn't believe us, we thought a little proof would help you understand. Miranda is one of those ghosts you don't believe in."

"Who does believe in ghosts?" Violet said, "You can't blame me."

"Maybe not, but maybe now you'll believe that we might be telling the truth," Amber said.

Violet looked around the room. "Where are you hiding the projectors?"

"What projectors?" Pekin asked.

"The projectors that conjured up that fake ghost," Violet said, scowling.

Amber threw up her hands. "Miranda, can you change clothes? Wear what Violet has on?"

Miranda disappeared and a moment later stood in the same blue cotton blouse hanging open over a white tank top and white capris that the skeptical visitor was wearing.

"Do you think a projector could do *that?*" Amber asked, matching Violet's scowl.

Violet's mouth hung open. She timidly stepped away from her dad. "So, okay, I believe you. What do you want me to do?"

"We'd like to summon Lily and let her see you and know you're okay. So she can be free to cross over," Mildew said.

"Okay, let's do it," Violet said.

"It might not be that simple," Mildew said. "First, Lily might not come out. Even if she does, she may not believe you're the baby she's searching for."

"Well, what are we supposed to do about that?" Violet asked.

*We can tell her to follow the silver thread*, Miranda said.

"What silver thread?" Ron asked.

"Miranda said there's a silver thread that connects Lily to Violet. That's how we found Violet's house in the first place."

Violet looked around her.

"You won't be able to see it," Mildew said. "Miranda's the only one of us who can. It's not for the living."

"This is getting weirder and weirder," Violet said.

"Tell us about it," Amber said. "We're kinda new at it as well."

"How do we get her to come to us?" Violet asked.

"Scout, can you help me move the bed over to the wall?" Mildew asked. "Ron, can you help?"

"Sure," Ron said. "What are we doing?"

"The most direct method for calling Lily is if we all sit in a circle. I'll light the white candle and we'll try to think her here."

"Think her here?" Ron asked, scratching his head.

"Opening our minds and asking her to join us."

"Aren't you afraid—" Violet started.

"Don't worry," Mildew said. "Before we start, I'll say a protection prayer to surround us in white light. Never attempt to contact the spirit world without protecting yourself."

"It sounds dangerous," Violet said, her face reflecting her nervousness.

"Most probably there's nothing to worry about, but I have to be honest. Anytime you summon a spirit there's the possibility a spirit other than the one you want will try to come through."

"What do we do if one does?" a clearly concerned Violet asked.

"There's every reason to think that won't happen," Mildew said. "Lily is not a vengeful spirit. She's a sad one. The prayer is a strong barrier to other entities." She patted Violet's shoulder. "I will make the prayer very specific. I truly don't expect that we'll encounter an evil spirit."

"Not totally comforting," Violet said.

"It might be a good idea for you to sit next to your dad," Scout said. "Since Lily will recognize him and may find it easier to believe you're her daughter."

It was snug, with knees touching, but all six managed to fit into a circle on the floor. Amber sat next to Violet, who was next to Rob, then Pekin, Scout and Mildew, who completed the circle. Mildew set the candle in the center and lit it.

"Let's all hold hands and close our eyes," she said. "I'll say the prayer of protection, and we can silently request Lily to come to us."

Once she'd prayed over the circle, asking for Lily's spirit to come through and asking for the white light to descend on them and cover them with divine protection from unwanted entities, Mildew said out loud, "Lily Grayson, we need you here. We seek to set you free from the earthly bonds that bind you to this place. Your daughter is here. Come to us and see."

Everyone in the circle silently asked Lily to come forth. When several minutes went by without the ghost appearing, Violet said, "I don't think this will work."

"Please, you need to remain silent and keep trying to summon her," Mildew said. "Keep your eyes closed."

Mildew cleared her throat and once again called for Lily to come. "Lily Grayson, we request your presence. Your daughter is here."

"It's so cold," Violet said after a moment.

"She's here," Mildew whispered.

A chill settled over the room and a breeze swirled around the people in the circle. An eerie voice said, *My baby. Where's my baby?* Ghostly sobs filled the air, and everyone's eyes opened.

"There," Amber whispered, pointing to the cradle, where a transparent figure floated.

"Lily?" Ron whispered in awe, his voice catching in his throat.

The ghost's hands reached into the cradle and she started to shriek. *Where's my baby?*

"She's here," Pekin said. "Your baby's here, but she's all grown up now." She pointed to Violet. "See?"

But the ghost didn't respond. It kept sobbing and calling for her baby over and over.

Pekin looked at Scout. "I'm sorry," she said. "I have to do this."

He nodded and squeezed her hand.

"Everyone close your eyes again," Mildew whispered, "so Pekin can summon her."

Everyone closed their eyes and called on Lily to join them. The room grew colder. Pekin squeezed her eyes shut and grew tense as she waited for the ghost to pop inside her.

"Eep!" sounded from Amber and Pekin's eyes flew open at the odd sound.

Amber was staring blankly into the circle, her eyes wide and unmoving.

"Amber," Pekin whispered, "what are you doing?"

Amber didn't respond. She sat up straighter, looking at nothing.

"Mildew," Pekin said, "what's happening?"

"Lily bonded with Amber," Mildew said.

Pekin's mouth fell open in disbelief as she watched her friend.

"Lily, are you there?" Mildew said to Amber.

*Why am I here?*

"Your daughter is in this room."

*Where is my baby?*

"Violet is right there," Mildew pointed. "She grew up."

*No. She's not my baby.*

"Lily, you died in childbirth in 1992. Violet is 26 years old now."

*No.*

Violet watched, fascinated.

"Talk to her," Mildew said to Violet.

Violet shivered, and said "Mom? It's me, Violet. Don't you know me?"

Amber's face turned toward Violet. *No. I want my baby.*

Miranda shimmered into view. *Lily, look at the thread. You can see that it connects you to your daughter, Violet.*

Amber's eyes searched the floor, following something only she could see, until she looked up at Violet. Amber reached out her hand and touched Violet's face.

Violet jerked away, then quickly said, "I'm sorry. I didn't mean to do that." She took Amber's hand. "I read what you wrote to me in my baby book...Mom. It meant a lot to me."

Amber's eyes filled with tears. *You're my baby? You're my baby.*

"Yes, Mom. I am."

*Can I hold you?*

Violet climbed to her feet and extended a hand to Amber to help her up. They looked at each other silently for a long minute until Violet moved into Amber's open arms. Both broke into tears, the sound of sobbing filling the room. After a moment, they pulled apart. Amber brushed Violet's hair back from her face, her hand lingering for an instant before it dropped to her side.

*Thank you for finding me*, Lily said. *I knew you'd be beautiful and wonderful and good.*

"I'm the lucky one," Violet said. "If you hadn't stayed here, I wouldn't have had the chance to meet you." She wiped at her eyes. "These kids made it happen. They were so worried about you being unable to move on. I wish I'd found you years ago, so you didn't have to endure such heartbreak and loneliness."

Ron cleared his throat and reached a hand toward Amber, tears in his eyes. "Lily. It's me, Ron."

She silently looked at him, her face not giving away what she was feeling at his presence.

"You were gone, Lily." His eyes were red-rimmed and his lips trembled. "I thought you were gone. I didn't know. I would have come back, even just to see you one more time."

She reached out and gently touched his cheek.

He brought his hand up to the spot her hand had been. "I'm so sorry I didn't know. Please forgive me, Lil."

*I understand. All is well now.*

Violet hugged her dad and then gripped Amber's arms.

"You must let go now, Mom. You belong in heaven, and I hope to see you again there one day. Don't hold onto the sadness keeping you trapped here on earth, when you should be with all your loved ones who've crossed over. I'll never forget you, Mother, but I want you to be in heaven."

Out of the corner of her eye, Pekin thought she saw a gray blur whisk by behind Amber, but when she blinked and looked again, there was nothing. She opened her mouth to ask if anyone else had noticed, but something was happening with Amber.

Amber backed away from Violet and looked toward a corner of the room. She smiled. Everyone watched as Lily's spirit left Amber's body and walked toward something only she could see. Lily glanced back at Violet. *I love you so much, and I'll be waiting for you.* Then she took another step and was gone.

Amber blinked. "What happened?" She looked down at her friends still sitting on the floor. "Lily didn't come, did she?" She turned to Violet. "I'm sorry nothing happened. Is it because I broke the circle and stood up? We need to try again, though. Maybe if we—"

"What are you talking about?" Violet said. "It worked."

"What?" Amber asked.

"Amber," Mildew said, climbing to her feet, "Lily was here. You helped her go into the light."

"I did?" Amber looked confused. "You mean Pekin did, right?"

"No," Pekin said, standing. "Lily used *you* to talk to Violet, not me."

"You're kidding, right?" Her hands flew to her face. "I feel kinda weird."

"You should," Scout said. "You've been sharing a body with a ghost." He took her arm and led her over to the bed. "You need to sit down."

Amber sank down on the bed. "Crap. I missed everything."

"No," Scout laughed. "You *were* everything."

"Well, I hope someone will tell me *everything* that happened."

"For sure," he said.

Mildew suggested going back to the family room, so they all made their way down the stairs. Spike had been running in circles at the bottom of the stairs, barking, and none of them had noticed. Scout stooped and picked him up. "Sorry, pal. We sorta forgot you were down here." He tucked the little guy under his arm as he dropped down on the couch, then set Spike in his lap and ruffled his fur. "It's all okay now, Spike. No more ghosts in this house."

Spike immediately nuzzled under Scout's arm and lay still.

"What about Miranda?" Amber whispered.

"Shush," Scout said with a grin. "Don't tell him."

# Chapter Twenty-Six

"SO, ARE YOU ALL RIGHT?" Mildew asked Violet.

"I'm speechless," Violet responded. "That was the oddest, most wonderful thing I've ever experienced. I met my mother, who's been dead since the day I was born."

"And you set her free," Pekin said.

"Can you believe it?" Violet asked, her face reflecting her amazement. She glanced at her father, who was sitting, cradling the baby book, the track of a lone tear on his cheek, and she squeezed his hand.

"What was it like?" Amber asked.

Violet looked at her, but didn't respond immediately. Instead, she grabbed Amber in a hug. "I'm sorry I was such a...a——"

"Witch?" Amber offered innocently.

"Yes. I'm sorry I was such a witch."

Amber grabbed her and hugged her back. "I'm just glad it worked out." She pulled away. "You turned out to be a nice person after all."

"I'm usually a nice person," Violet said.

"Well, I'm sorry I wasn't very nice to you," Amber said.

"All is forgiven. Right?"

"Right." Amber grinned. "So, what was it like?"

"It was unbelievable. I saw a ghost!"

"Two ghosts, actually."

"What you said to Lily was great," Ron said, his wedding album under his arm. "You made her feel like you really loved her."

"You know what's weird? I felt it. I *do* really love her."

"But—"

"I don't understand it either. I mean, I read her notes to her baby...to me, and I could feel the love from her when she was in Amber, and I *knew* her. It was like a primal thing, and I felt deep love."

"Are you sad now?" Amber asked.

"No. Not really. I won't really miss her because I never had her in the first place. And, even though I felt an attachment when I finally was faced with her, I let her go. I know it was the right thing to do and I'm glad I could do it for her. I think I feel happy."

"It's too bad we're kids," Amber said. "This seems like the kind of occasion where we should all toast our success."

"Should we all toast with a soda?" Pekin asked. "I think we have a bunch in the fridge."

"Works for me," Scout said.

"You guys?" Pekin asked Ron and Violet.

"Sure," Ron said, and Violet nodded.

"I'll be back in a minute," Pekin said, heading for the

kitchen. "Scout, you want to help me?"

Scout joined her and got out the sodas while Pekin found glasses. Actual champagne glasses. She spun around holding one. "Ta da!"

She and Scout filled six glasses with Sprite. Pekin picked up two, but, before she could leave the kitchen, Scout said, "Pekin. Hold up."

She looked at him questioningly.

He took the glasses out of her hands and set them on the counter.

"I just wanted to tell you I'm glad it turned out the way it did. I was worried."

"I'm happy you worry about me." She looked up at him and he pulled her into a hug. "I didn't feel good about doing something that you didn't really want me to do. I'm glad I didn't have to." She rested her head on his shoulder. "But—"

"I know. I trust you, Pekie, and if it's something you think you need to do, I'll always be there to catch you."

"Thanks, Scoutie." She flashed him a big, grateful smile.

"We good?" he asked.

"We're better than good," Pekin said, picking up the glasses. "Let's go toast."

When everyone had a glass of bubbly, Scout held up his glass. "Amber, why don't you make the toast, since it was your idea."

She giggled and lifted her glass. "To another successful spirit rescue."

"I'd like to make a toast, too," Violet said. She lifted her glass and said, a catch in her voice, "To my mother."

Everyone solemnly clinked glasses and drank.

When the glasses were empty, Violet said, "We should get on the road. I hate to be away from Hailey too long."

"Who's Hailey?" Amber asked.

"She's my eighteen-month-old daughter."

"Oh, too big for the cradle then."

"That she is," Violet said with a chuckle. "The cradle is a piece of art which Hailey can put her dolls in. At least until I have another baby to sleep in it."

"Aww, that's such a great idea," Amber said. "Do you have any pictures of her?"

"I do!" Violet said, pulling out her phone and scrolling through her photos.

"Here's one from last week. She's such a cute age right now." She handed the phone to Amber. Pekin and Scout and Mildew crowded around to admire the picture of the little blonde toddler, curls bouncing around her face and a whale spout ponytail on the top of her head.

"She's so *cuuute!*" Amber said.

"You'll have to…" Violet paused and looked at her dad. "You'll have to come meet her sometime."

"Really?" Amber's eyes widened. "You'd want to see us again?"

"You gave me a remarkable experience. One I'll never forget. I'd love to see you all again."

After hugs all around, Violet and Ron headed for home.

# Chapter Twenty-Seven

"I'M SO TIRED," Amber said, sinking down on the couch.

"I'm not surprised," Mildew said. "It's not easy to host a ghost."

"*Host a ghost.* I like it!" Amber said.

"Why did Lily choose Amber?" Pekin asked. "I thought it would be me. I was all psyched up for it."

"I couldn't help it," Amber said meekly.

"Don't get your nose out of joint, Pekie," Scout said. "It doesn't mean she liked Amber better than you."

"What? My nose isn't—"

Scout grabbed her with one arm and ruffled her hair with the other hand. "Just kidding."

She pulled away in a huff. Hands on her hips, she glared at him. Then she doubled over in giggles. "Me, too."

"I'm glad you're kidding," Amber said. "I was starting to feel bad."

"You have no reason to feel badly," Mildew said. "You saved the day."

"Yeah, but it wasn't because of anything *I* did. It just *happened* to me."

"I admit I'm surprised it worked out that way," Mildew said. "I guess you've got more sensitivity than we thought."

"Well, I *have* been working on my meditation," Amber responded.

Mildew patted her hand. "It's working quite well for you, I would say."

Amber beamed.

"It's official, I guess," Scout said. "I'm the only one who doesn't have *it*."

"What's 'it'?" Pekin asked.

"I don't know, but apparently you and Amber have it."

"On the other hand, we've only had two ghost jobs, so maybe your time's coming. You got that meditation thing working for you pretty fast."

He laughed. "I'm still just kidding. I'm fine if I never *host a ghost.*"

"Do you have any questions, Amber?" Mildew said.

"I just don't understand what happened. I mean, I know what happened but I didn't feel anything. It was like I was asleep or something."

"Well, you were pushed aside to make room for Lily to control your body."

"But, can any ghost just pop in there any time? Like I could be walking down the street and suddenly I could be at the mall and I wouldn't know how I got there?"

"That's very unlikely," Mildew said. "It takes a lot of energy for a spirit to be able to inhabit someone. They can't just willy-nilly settle into someone walking down the street and take over. If that were possible, you'd see zombie-like people stumbling around town. I don't believe you need to worry about that happening to you again. But, if I were you, I'd say a protection prayer every day." She laughed. "Couldn't hurt."

"Did you guys——" Pekin started, then looked at her hands.

"Did we what?" Mildew said.

"I thought I saw something up there, when Lily was in Amber."

"Something?" Scout asked.

"But I blinked and it was gone, so maybe it was nothing."

"Like what?" Mildew asked.

"It was kind of a blur. I saw it…or thought I did. I'm sure it was nothing."

"I didn't see anything," Scout said.

Mildew was quiet. "It was probably nothing." But her eyes were suddenly hooded.

Before Pekin could say anything more, there was a shimmer in the room and Miranda appeared. She was dressed like Amber in jeans and a tank top.

"You look good, Miranda," Amber said with a big grin.

*If I could, I would fix them for you*, Miranda said.

"Fix what?" Amber asked.

*Your dungarees. They have holes in them, like your knees are coming out. I know how to sew, but I can't make a needle work in your world.*

Amber laughed, her hand covering her mouth, her shoulders shaking.

*What?* Miranda looked confused.

"Miranda," Pekin said, "Amber's jeans aren't torn. Well, I guess they are, but they're supposed to look that way. It's a *thing.*"

*But why would someone want to wear clothes with holes?*

"Because everyone wears them," Pekin said. "It's a fashion statement. But, I have to agree with you. I never understood why people like holey clothes."

"Because they're *cool*," Amber said.

"That's a matter of opinion," Mildew said. "I'm with Pekin on this one. I don't like holes. They make me cringe."

"You don't like my shredded T-shirt?" Amber asked.

"It's not my favorite," Pekin said. "But, you do you and I'll do me."

*What does that mean?* Miranda asked.

"It means, if Amber likes holey clothes, it's her choice. And if I don't like them, I don't have to wear them."

"Besides," Amber said to Miranda, "you dressed like me, so maybe it'll grow on you."

*What will grow on me?*" Miranda looked horrified.

"That means maybe you'll decide you like that look," Pekin said.

"You've got a lot to learn, Miranda, if you're going to hang around the twenty-first century." Amber couldn't suppress her grin. "But we'll be happy to teach you."

*Oh, yes. But, first, I have to fix these holes.* She shimmered, and, when all was clear, her jeans no longer had rips and tears.

"*Sooo* much better," Pekin said. Amber just huffed.

"Well, I should be going," Mildew said. "All that's left is

for you to give your final report to the Dwyers. Everything turned out the way it should have."

Amber hugged Mildew. "It was amazing. Can't wait for the next one."

Mildew smiled and waved goodbye as she stepped out the door, leaving the kids to flop down on the couch in the family room. Pekin couldn't decide if Mildew looked troubled when she left, but she couldn't suppress a shiver as her eyes traveled to the stairwell.

"You okay, Pekie?" Scout asked.

"I'm fine," she responded, pasting a smile on her face.

"I'm tired," Amber said, throwing her head against the back of the sofa, dramatically flinging her arms out. "Oops. Sorry," she said when her flying arm smacked Scout.

"No prob," he said.

"Well, I'm famished," Pekin said.

"Me, too," Scout piped in. "Want to go to Benny's for burgers?"

It was unanimous, and the perfect ending to a successful day.

# Chapter Twenty-Eight

～～～～～～～～～～～～～～～～～～～～～～～～～～～～～～

"I GUESS WE DON'T have to stay here anymore," Pekin said. "The Dwyers will be back day after tomorrow."

"We don't have to," Scout said, "but I don't want to leave Spike here by himself." He ruffled the fur on the little dog's head. Spike's wagging tail wiggled his whole body. "Speaking of which, I'm going to take him out."

When Scout and Spike got back, Pekin said, "Amber and I talked it over. If you're staying, we're staying, too."

"But we're going home tomorrow morning to spend a little time with our families," Amber said. "We can come back here in the afternoon and then all go to dinner together."

"I guess we can all sleep in our own bedrooms upstairs tonight," Scout said. "Since the house isn't haunted anymore."

"We *could*," Pekin said, "but it's been fun when we're all together down here. Like a slumber party."

Scout rolled his eyes. "Easy for you to say, since you and Amber are sleeping on the couch."

"I thought you said the recliner was comfortable," Pekin said.

"It's marginally better than the floor," he said.

"Oh, you've survived so far. You can suck it up for a couple of more nights," Amber said.

"Okay. Whatever you ladies want."

"You know what I think?" Amber said. "I think we should have a double date tomorrow night. I'll invite Josh over and we can order a pizza."

"And watch scary movies?" Pekin asked.

"We have *enough* scary in our lives," Scout said. "Let's watch an *Avengers* movie."

"Ooh," Amber said. "I like those."

For the first time in a week, the kids weren't on edge, worried about failing their task. They'd successfully helped Lily cross over.

"We've had an action-packed few weeks," Scout said.

"And we're all still here," Amber said. "Even me."

"You guys really stepped up," Pekin said. "We're a good team."

"Do you think we'll have to host ghosts every time?" Amber asked.

"I hope not," Pekin said. "Although Scout probably wants a turn."

"That would be a negative," he responded. "After seeing how much fun it was for you two, I think I'll give it a pass."

"I'm ready for a good old-fashioned normal ghost," Pekin said. "Like Casper."

"Miranda's kind of like Casper," Amber said. "She's friendly and she likes us." She yawned. "I'd love to keep chatting with you guys, but I'm totally wiped out. Can we call it a night?"

"I'm with you," Pekin said, stretching. "We could all use the rest."

# Chapter Twenty-Nine

~~~~~~~~~~~~~~~~~~~~~~~~~~~~~~~~~~~~~~~~~~~~~~~~~~~~~~~~~~~~~~~~

A FTER SLEEPING LIKE A ROCK, Pekin was the first to wake up. She smiled when she spotted Scout, looking comfortable in the recliner, little Spike tucked in at his side, his head resting on Scout's chest.

When she looked at her phone, she was surprised to see it was after ten.

"Wake up, you guys. It's really late and I'm hungry."

Amber rolled over and pulled the blanket over her head. Scout stretched and Spike lifted his head and yawned, then hopped off the recliner and trotted over to stand by the front door. He gave a little yip-yip and bounced up and down in a circle when no one immediately rushed over to take him out.

Pekin leaned over and grabbed the blanket, jerking it down despite Amber's protestations. "Get up, sleepyhead. Don't you want breakfast?"

"No. I want to sleep."

"Yumm. Pancakes. Waffles. *Bacon!*"

"You go get ready. I'll get up when you're done," Amber mumbled from under the pillow she'd pulled over her head.

"But—"

"Only two bathrooms. One for you and one for Scout." She curled up in a fetal position. "I promise I'll be up when you get out."

"Okay, but we're not waiting very long if you're not. Scout wants breakfast, too." She glanced at Scout, who was sitting up in the recliner. "Right, Scout?"

"You had me at *bacon*."

"Are you cooking?" Amber asked Pekin.

"Have you met me? I vote for Benny's."

Amber sat up, rubbing her eyes, her auburn hair forming a messy strawberry halo around her head. "Scout," she said, "I think your little buddy needs to go out."

"Yeah, I got that. His hints are hard to miss. I guess you can use *my* bathroom, Amber, since I'll be on a walk with Spikey for the next fifteen minutes."

"All *right*. If you guys are in such a hurry, I'll get up."

"Breakfast, breakfast," Pekin sang as she hopped up the stairs to the bathroom next to the master bedroom.

Amber clambered off the couch and grabbed the tote containing her toiletries. "Don't leave without me."

Scout laughed and shut the door behind him and Spike.

The hot water of the shower disguised a sudden chill that settled over the bathroom. But, feeling like something was a little off-kilter, Amber shivered and peeked her head around the shower curtain. The air seemed colder than when she'd started her shower, but shampoo was suddenly running into Amber's eyes and she pulled her head back in the shower and stuck her head under the spray. By the time she turned off the water, she'd forgotten it had even happened.

AMBER HEARD JOSH'S CAR when it pulled up to the curb in front of the house, and she rushed to the front door.

"Geez, Amber. It's not like you didn't just see Josh a couple of days ago," Pekin said with a smile.

Amber stuck out her tongue and giggled. "Oh, hush."

She jumped into Josh's arms when he walked through the door. "I've missed you."

Pekin made fake gagging noises and laughed at Josh's comical expression as he hugged Amber.

Scout clapped him on the back. "Hey, bro. You missed all the action. You'd be proud of your girl."

"Can't wait to hear the all the details," Josh said, one arm draped over Amber's shoulders.

Before they could sit down, the doorbell rang, announcing the arrival of the pizza.

Scout paid the pizza guy and carried the boxes into the kitchen, Pekin, Amber and Josh following the aroma of pepperoni into the kitchen.

Scout plopped two slices of pineapple pizza on a paper plate, and Josh took two more slices of the same.

"Good stuff," Scout said around a bite.

"I can't believe you guys like pineapple on your pizza," Amber said.

"Um, yeah," Josh said, knocking his elbow against Scout's with a grin.

"You guys don't know what you're missing," Scout said. "You go on and have boring old everyday pepperoni. Josh and I think outside the box."

"Ours is better," Amber said. "You don't need to save us any slices of yours."

Once everyone was on a third slice, the kids filled Josh in on their successful result in the Lily Grayson case.

"It was me," Amber said with a big smile. "Lily jumped into me and I didn't even know what was going on because my brain was shoved aside by Lily."

Josh looked at her like she'd sprouted a second head.

"It's true," she said. "I became Lily, and then Lily could talk to her daughter and hug her and everything. I mean, I hugged her daughter, but it was really Lily."

"That's making my head spin," Josh said. He took her hand. "Are you all right?"

"I'm fine. It made me tired, but I got a lot of sleep last night so I'm okay today." She squeezed his hand. "Thanks for worrying about me."

"I can relate," Scout said. "I was freaked when Pekin was invaded by a ghost. Even thinking about it now…"

"Yeah. I don't blame you, bro," Josh said. "It's kinda weird."

"It is *not*." Amber glared at her boyfriend.

"I didn't mean it in a *bad* way, babe," Josh said, squeezing her hand.

"Not just *anyone* can host a ghost," Amber said with a huff.

"Huh?" Josh asked.

"That's what we call it now. Host a Ghost. It's a thing."

"Not sure it's a *thing*," Scout said. "Yet. It's only happened twice."

"But twice out of our only two cases," Pekin said. "Amber does deserve the credit."

Scout shrugged.

"If it happens again, in our next case, then you'll have to admit it's a thing," Pekin said.

He put his arm around Pekin's shoulders and pulled her against him on the couch. "Who knew having ghostbusters for girlfriends would be so nuts?" he asked Josh.

Pekin's face turned bright red. She was pleased and embarrassed. She wasn't quite as comfortable as Amber was with such open displays of boyfriend/girlfriend affection. She was just getting used to the whole idea of her and Scout, and now they were sitting on the couch, make that *snuggling* on the couch, with another couple. Even if that other couple was Amber and Josh. When she glanced around and found that no one had noticed her embarrassment, she relaxed against Scout, and allowed herself to feel wonder at finding herself in an actual relationship with the boy of her dreams.

"I think this whole ghost thing is really cool," Josh said. "Wish I'd thought of it."

"It's not something you just think of and go out and do," Pekin said, sitting forward on the couch, her arms resting on her knees. "You have to actually be able to contact ghosts. Not everyone can."

"Well, Scout and I didn't think we could contact ghosts," Amber said.

"But you took it seriously. You didn't do it just because you thought it was cool. If I remember correctly, you thought it was the farthest thing from cool."

"You made me do it," Amber pouted.

"Yeah. I guess I did," Pekin said. She turned to Josh. "Sorry. I didn't mean to discourage you. I mean, I'm sure Amber would love to have you find ghosts with her."

"I was mostly kidding," Josh said. "I mean, I do think it's cool, but it's your thing. And Amber's. I'm happy to hear the stories, but I don't need to be in the same room with a ghost. That shimmery thing in the hallway upstairs was enough for me."

He looked down at Amber. "Is that okay with you, babe?"

She snuggled up under his arm. "It's okay if you're scared."

"I never said I was scared." Josh pulled away. "I was *not* scared."

"JK," Amber said.

"JK?" he asked.

"Just Kidding."

"Well, glad that's settled," Pekin said. "I mean, we're just a small start-up, after all."

"Huh?" Scout asked, tilting his head.

"Pekie! Quit dissing my boyfriend." Amber's eyes flashed.

She smacked her forehead. "Sorry. I'm digging the hole deeper, aren't I?" She sighed. "I just meant we're the right size with the three of us."

"Should we watch the movie?" Scout asked. He stood, picked up the empty pizza box and turned to Josh. "Here's the deal. We love you, bro. You can come help us on a case anytime you want. Amber, your boyfriend is always welcome. Pekie...stop digging."

He looked over his shoulder and winked at her as he carried the pizza box into the kitchen. He didn't return for a few minutes, and popping sounds came from the kitchen.

Carrying a big bowl of popcorn, he said, "Movie time!" and plopped down on the couch next to Pekin, setting the bowl on the coffee table.

"Everything's perfect now," Amber said, settling back under Josh's arm.

*It kind of is*, Pekin thought, aware of Scout's heart beating, and the warmth of his arm around her shoulders, how comfortable she felt leaning against him. She was scarcely aware of the movie until partway through, content to bask in the wonder of Scout next to her. She snuck a look at his face, which was intent on the movie until he must have felt her gaze, as he smiled and ruffled her hair.

Pekin sighed happily and finally paid attention to the movie.

# CHAPTER THIRTY

SATURDAY MORNING found the kids once again at Benny's. They wanted to get breakfast out of the way, then do a sweep and pick up around the Firefly Lane house to make sure they left it in as good condition as they found it.

"Are you nervous," Scout asked Pekin. "You know, with the Dwyers on their way back?"

"Nope. I feel pretty good. We were able to send Lily into the light and their house is no longer haunted. I can't wait to tell them all about it."

"They're going to be so happy!" Amber said.

"They don't get home until late afternoon," Pekin said. "Should we make dinner for them? They'll probably be tired from traveling."

"What kind of dinner?" Amber asked. "My skills in the kitchen are limited."

"Mine are, too," Pekin said. "I can make grilled cheese and order pizza. Maybe we should forget making dinner."

"Or," Scout said, "we could barbeque burgers and hot dogs. They have a really cool grill in the backyard."

"Do you know how?" Pekin asked.

"Oh, yeah. My dad always puts me in charge when we're grilling. Piece of cake."

"Wow," Pekin said. "I have a boyfriend who can cook."

"Grill." Scout laughed. "I said *grill*."

"I'll text them and see if they're up to it," Pekin said. "Maybe they just want their home to themselves and we can fill them in tomorrow." She tapped away on her phone.

In moments, the phone dinged. "They're in! They said a barbeque would be wonderful."

They spent the afternoon shopping and preparing for the evening meal. Onions chopped, patties formed, tomatoes sliced.

While they waited for the Dwyers to get home, Scout was hunched over his laptop. "How does this look?" he said, carrying his computer into the kitchen. Pekin put the paring knife down and rinsed her hands. "What have you got there?"

"I've been working on our *Spirit Investigation Report*. I figured it would be good to have it ready for the Dwyers when they get home."

Pekin scanned the page. "It looks so professional!"

"I've been fooling around with a format. I made a template we can use for all our cases. It has headings like Client, Address, Date, Entity, Resolution, Notes. If you think of any others we need, they'll be easy to add. When I get home, I'll fill one out for Elonia Collins for the Elmwood case and let you review it."

"You sound like a real businessman," Amber said. "I feel so professional."

Pekin laughed. "I like it. Thanks for remembering to do that."

"They have a printer upstairs, so I'll print it out for them and make an extra copy for us."

"Great," Pekin said. "I'll buy a notebook for us to file them all in."

After the report was printed and left on the dining room table, Scout played with Spike and took him for a long walk while Pekin and Amber performed a room search to make sure everything was in the same condition as their first day on the job.

# Chapter Thirty-One

S PIKE WAS THE FIRST to know when his masters arrived. He was hopping and whining at the front door when it swung open.

"Hello!" Edie called out when she stepped through the door.

Scout rushed forward to help with the luggage.

As the guys went about lugging the bags inside and up the stairs, Edie looked apprehensively at Pekin. "Did you... were you able to help our ghost move on?"

"Yes!" Amber blurted out, unable to hold back her excitement. "It was so cool the way it happened."

"Why don't you sit down and we'll tell you all about it?" Pekin said. "Amber, I think you're the best one to tell the story."

"Let's wait for Archie," Edie said. "Although I can hardly wait."

"I'm here," Archie called, followed down the stairs by Scout.

"We have a *Spirit Investigation Report* for you," Pekin said. "You can read it and file it away. But we'll still tell you all about what happened while you were gone."

When they were all settled in the family room, Amber stood and cleared her throat. "Lily is finally at rest."

"Lily?" Edie tilted her head.

"Oh, yeah. Claire Masterson told us the story. Windy is actually Lily Grayson. She was Ron Grayson's wife."

"I remember the name. That's who we bought the house from," Archie said.

"What happened is, Lily died in childbirth here in your house. Ron took the baby, Violet, and moved away after a few months. That's why Lily was looking all over for her baby. She didn't know she'd died, or that Ron had taken Violet and moved away."

"That's very sad," Edie said. "How did you get her to leave?"

"We tracked down Ron and convinced him to bring Violet here," Pekin said.

"Lily must have been so happy to see her daughter," Edie said.

"You'd think so," Amber said, "She didn't believe Violet was her daughter because she was looking for a baby. But then," Amber said dramatically, "Lily jumped into my body and got to talk to Violet in person."

"Wait. She jumped into you?"

"Well, we had to do a séance first."

"A séance?" Edie looked taken aback.

"Yeah. Kind of one. I'm not sure it was a real one since we sat on the floor and not around a table."

"How did you know what to do?"

"Our friend Mildew came and helped us when we couldn't get Lily to talk to us."

"Mildew?"

"Yep. Her name is really Mildred, but everyone calls her Mildew. She's kind of our mentor."

"I see," Edie said. "But I don't understand why, just because Lily jumped into you—"

"We call it hosting a ghost," Amber said.

"Okay. Still, I don't understand why Lily suddenly knew to do that."

"Well, Miranda told us there's a silver thread that connects ghosts to someone they're attached to on this plane. So, once Lily was in Amber's body, we told her to look at the thread."

"We couldn't see it but she could," Pekin added.

"Anyway, when Lily spotted the thread and saw where it led, she recognized her daughter and she and Violet talked and then they hugged and Lily said goodbye and went into the light."

Amber looked around at her audience. "Any questions?"

Pekin giggled. "You sound like a teacher."

Amber laughed.

"Is Miranda still here?" Edie asked. "We'd love to meet her. If we could."

"If she's around," Pekin said. To the air, she added, "Miranda, someone here would like to meet you. Can you come out?"

"Oh!" Edie exclaimed when a shimmer appeared in the room. "Is that her?" she whispered.

"Yes. You'll see in a moment."

Miranda became fully visible. *I'm here.*

"Miranda, this is Edie and Archie. They wanted to meet you."

*Hello. Very nice to meet you.*

Edie covered her mouth with her hand, momentarily stunned.

"Very nice to meet you, too," Archie said, glancing at his wife.

"Oh, yes," Edie said. "I'm sorry. I was just...startled. Miranda, we'd like to thank you for helping our Windy get closure. Lily, I mean."

*I'm happy she was able to be free.*

"How funny," Archie said. "Miranda is dressed just like Pekin." He cleared his throat. "I'm sorry. I didn't mean to offend you."

Miranda floated next to Pekin, their denim shorts and yellow tank tops identical.

"She always does that," Amber said. "She's more comfortable than when she's wearing the taffeta dress she was murdered in." She glanced at Miranda. "Sorry, Miranda."

*I no longer have any connection to the remains left behind. I'm not offended.*

"What do you think of today's world?" Archie asked the ghost.

*It's loud and colorful and people say anything. Not so polite anymore.*

"That pretty much sums it up," Archie agreed. "But

you'll still find good people who'll give you the shirt off their back if you need it."

"Miranda's so different from when we first met her," Amber said. "She was really shy and timid. Now she's out there exploring everything."

"And she's not afraid of appearing to people," Pekin said. "She doesn't make the lights flicker anymore."

"She made the lights flicker?" Edie asked.

"She sure did. When she was nervous or afraid."

*Can I go now?* Miranda asked.

"Oh, sure," Pekin said. "The Dwyers just wanted to meet you."

With Pekin's permission, Miranda disappeared.

"Oh, my." Edie put a hand to her chest. "Our ghost never spoke with us. And your ghost was so nice."

"We like her," Amber said.

Scout placed his hands on the table and stood. "Is it time to get the barbeque started?"

He got a unanimous response, and everyone followed him out to the backyard as Pekin and Amber brought out the burger patties and hotdogs and everything to go with them.

At the end of the meal, Scout asked if he could take Spike for a walk before they left. At the word "walk," the little terrier raced to the front door, stumpy tail wagging his whole body, and gave a huff, as if to say "hurry up."

"He really bonded with Spike while you were gone," Pekin said. "He's going to miss him."

"Does Scout have a dog at home?" Edie asked.

"No. I don't think he knew he liked them that much."

"We should get him one," Amber said. "For a surprise."

"I'm not sure his parents would appreciate that kind of surprise," Edie said. "Dogs are a lot of work. If you're going to have one, you need to be prepared to spend a lot of time with it, or it will be sad and lonely. Probably best to ask first before you surprise someone with a living creature."

"I didn't think of that," Amber said. "We'll definitely ask him instead of surprising him."

Of course, the moment Scout came in the front door, Amber burst out, "We think you should get a dog."

Pekin rolled her eyes.

"We'll go to the pound with you and help pick it out," Amber continued. "If you want."

Scout, who was bent over unhooking Spike's leash, finally focused on what Amber was saying.

"We were just going to go get you one," Amber blurted, "but Edie said we should tell you first."

"Wait, what?" Scout asked, a quizzical expression on his face.

"You know. A dog."

He raised his hands to ward Amber off. "I don't need a dog."

"But—"

"In a year, I'm going off to college. What happens to the dog then?"

Pekin glared at Amber. "That's what Edie was trying to tell you. Scout would probably drop the dog off at your house when he left for college."

"You can always come visit Spike," Archie said. "He's taken quite a shine to you."

Scout smiled. "Thanks. I just might." Then he nodded his head toward the door and said, "Are we ready to go?" He picked up his duffle bag which was sitting by the front door and looked expectantly at his friends. When Pekin and Amber joined him by the door, he said, "Thanks for the offer, Archie. I might do that."

"We really enjoyed meeting you," Pekin said. "We're happy everything worked out for your ghost. If you need our help in the future, please give us a call."

With a warm smile, Edie gave the three friends a hug and waved goodbye, Archie at her side, as they piled into Scout's car.

Once they pulled away from the curb, Amber said, "You can name him Sparky."

"Don't start, Amber," Scout said. "I'm not getting a dog."

"For now," she said under her breath.

# Chapter Thirty-Two

~~~~~~~~~~~~~~~~~~~~~~~~~~~~~~~~~~~~~~~~~~~~~~~~~~~~~~~~~~~~~~~~~~~~~~~~~~~

A T AMBER'S HOUSE, Scout carried her bag up to the door. As he turned back to his car, Amber said, "See you guys tomorrow."

Pekin leaned out the open window. "Amber, we've had too much togetherness. Let's take a break."

"Okay," Amber called. "See you day after tomorrow." She stuck out her tongue comically and carried her bag inside.

"Alone at last," Scout said as he slid into the driver's seat. He picked up Pekin's hand and leaned over to give her a quick kiss.

"It was kinda nice," she said. "You know. Being with you for a week."

"Thanks," he said. "I liked it, too."

"Two successful jobs," Pekin said. "Can you believe it?"

"I admit I was skeptical at first, but we killed it, didn't we?"

"We did!" She looked out the window. "I wonder what our next job will be."

"I wouldn't mind taking a break from that for a while, either."

"But—"

"I just mean, it's been an intense month for us. Let's have fun for a little while before we jump back in."

When he parked in front of her house, Scout said, "On the other hand, that intense month brought us together. We might never have been honest with each other about our feelings if—"

She squeezed his hand. "I know. I guess we owe it all to George Trent."

He laughed. "I can't believe you just said that."

She looked out the window. "I can't believe I did either."

Scout pulled her bag from the back seat and carried it up to the front door.

"Hey, Pekie," he called over his shoulder as she was closing the car door. "There's something here for you."

She hurried up the walk to the porch. A Manila envelope with her name on it sat propped against the door.

"What is it?" she asked.

"I don't know," Scout said. "Open it."

She picked the package up and slid her finger under the sealed flap. She turned the envelope upside down and a key fell into her hand. She held it up and examined it.

"Do you know what that's for?" Scout asked.

"No clue."

"Is that all there is?" he asked.

Pekin handed him the key and opened the envelope wider. "No. There's something else in here. She pulled out a plastic sandwich bag, and tucked the Manila envelope under her arm. She unzipped the sandwich bag and reached inside.

"Oh, my God," she said as she removed five one hundred dollar bills.

There was a yellow sticky on one of the bills that said, "DEPOSIT" and then "Talk soon. Matt Cooley."

"Here we go again," Scout said.

Pekin shot him a sympathetic look. She understood his disappointment. "Maybe it—"

She stopped, her eye catching a fleeting movement over Scout's shoulder, but when she peered around him, there was nothing...except a gray blur that was blinking out of sight.

# ACKNOWLEDGMENTS

I want to give my heartfelt thanks to everyone who believes in me. My family near and far who are always willing to help me as I trudge through the days, weeks, *words*, it takes to write a book. I'm so blessed to be surrounded by friends and family who offer encouragement and praise, and often read more than one draft of whichever book is my current project.

My sister, Sheila Baldwin, deserves special thanks, as she's there every step of the way making sure whatever I need appears whenever I need it. Seriously, Sheila, I couldn't do it without you. My sister, Michelle Hutton, has read just about everything I've written, often more than once, and is excellent at finding overlooked typos and other mistakes I missed in my own rereading. I'm always excited to see what she thinks, and love that she's willing to forego her own reading list to fit in my drafts.

Many thanks to Elise and Maya Crocker for thoughtful edits and help with understanding the teen mind. And thank you, Elise, for asking thought-provoking questions to help me flesh out my ideas.

My friend Mike Oldham offered a few helpful suggestions that I actually used. So many friends and family have cheered me along. Kind words and encouragement count for so much. They make me feel special!

My thanks also to my wonderful editor, Shelly Stinchcomb, Debra Kennedy, who formatted my novels, Dane at eBook Launch for the incredible cover art, Acorn Publishing, and the Acorn team, Jessica Therrien, Holly Kammier and Lacey Impellizeri, all of whom helped pave my path to publication.

And, lastly, thanks to everyone who leaves me a review. Those reviews on Amazon, Goodreads and other spots just might tempt someone to read my books!

IF YOU HAVEN'T READ IT YET
BE SURE TO CHECK OUT
# THE HAUNTING OF ELMWOOD MANOR
THE FIRST BOOK IN THE
PEKIN DEWLAP SERIES

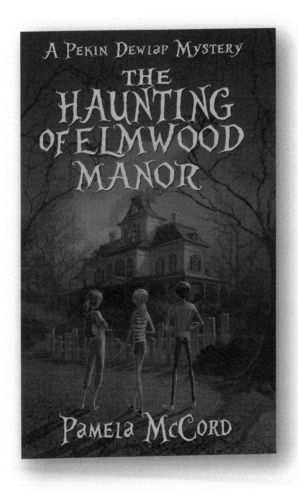

Available on:

- **Amazon**
- **Barnes and Noble**
- **most other major online retailers**

Made in the USA
Middletown, DE
04 June 2024

55238803R00135